A Second Chance for Love

Gaylene Nunn

Weezie Publishing

Contents

Then the woman surprises him again when he says she probably expects an apology from him. She remembers Ender's words about being a busy, important man and says she doesn't expect an apology from a man like him. However, when she asks why he's in Miami, he replies on business and gets a typical sarcastic response from her. Next, she nearly pushed her plate off the table. Then, she got up and left with the ocean breeze catching her fragrance and blowing it right into his face.

Ender inhales deeply and looks down at the table. He rubs his forehead, remembering he spent months trying to find out what the fragrance was. Finally, Ender and a woman whose name he can't remember visited a botanical garden in Istanbul. It was there he found out it was jasmine. Ender vowed to himself if he ever saw the woman again, he would know her by the smell of jasmine and the amber sparks that explode from her angry eyes. Out of all the women in the world and all the places Ender had visited in the past two years, he finally came into contact with her again. Closing his eyes, Ender can still picture her lying on his bed and him bending down to kiss her perfect lips.

Chapter 1

Valerie

Visiting Istanbul has been on Valerie's bucket list since she was a little girl, and it has finally happened. Yes, it took five years to save enough money for the trip, but it has been a fantastic experience. She has three days left before going home and a lot more to see. Valerie stands gazing at a Picasso hanging in the Sakip Sabanci Museum in Istanbul, Turkey. She muses that the painting is breathtaking and well worth the unplanned trip to the museum on the opposite side of town from her hotel.

Valerie takes a step back, turning at the same time. Unfortunately, a giant of a man bumps into her, causing her to fall on the hard floor with her left ankle underneath her. "Oh, my gosh! My ankle," Valerie says aloud.

"Sir," the man says, looking at another man instead of addressing Valerie.

"What is it, Joseph?" another man asks sharply. Valerie looks up at the owner of the harsh voice. He is a handsome man with reddish-blond hair. His square jaw is sporting a four-day-old beard, but it's his eyes that catch Valerie's attention. They are hazel and hard, and she nicknames him Hard Eyes in her mind.

"Sir, I bumped into this woman," the man named Joseph says. "What should I do?"

"Nothing. She can get up on her own. We are late and need to go," Hard Eyes replies.

"Now, wait just a minute," Valerie speaks up, staring at hard eyes. "I've hurt my ankle and need help to get up."

"Very well. Joseph, help her up and onto the bench over there." Hard Eyes lifts his arm and points to a bench across the room. "Hurry."

Joseph helps Valerie to her feet, but she wobbles, unable to put any weight on her left ankle. As hard eyes watches, Joseph helps Valerie to the bench.

Valerie mutters a thank you to the man named Joseph and turns her attention to hard eyes. "Well, are you just going to stand there, or are you going to help me?" she demands.

Hard Eyes stares at Valerie and stands in front of her. "Lady, do you know who I am?"

"No, and I don't care who you are. I'm injured. What are you going to do about it?"

Hard Eyes gets into his pocket and pulls out some money. "Here is the fare for the taxi," he says, handing the cash to Valerie.

Valerie looks at him in disbelief and pushes his hand away. "I don't want your money, you pompous idiot." She hears Joseph snicker and watches as Hard Eyes gives him a shriveling look. Joseph appears to shrink a foot. "I need help."

"Look, lady. I'm a very busy, important man. I don't have time to stand here and argue with you. Take the money for the taxi and go to a doctor if your ankle hurts that bad." Hard Eyes' face is turning a bright shade of red, signaling his anger.

Valerie stares into his eyes. "A decent human being would help, especially since I'm not from here and do not know where to find a doctor."

"Lady, what do you want me to do?"

"Well, if you're half as important as you think you are, you should know a doctor and take me there," Valerie replies.

Hard Eyes rolls his eyes and huffs out a breath of air, showing his disapproval. "Very well. Joseph, find Azra and inform her I am delayed. Tell her I will call her later and explain."

"Yes sir," Joseph replies, leaving Valerie, Hard Eyes, and another large, bulky man.

"Burak, pull the car around to the front of the building. This woman and I will meet you at the door," Hard Eyes says.

Chapter 2

Ender

O f all the times to be running late, Ender contemplates as he walks fast. Of course, Azra will be furious that he's late for the engagement party for her sister. But, at least I've made it to the museum, now to get quickly through these commoners milling around.

When he hears Joseph say, sir, I bumped into this woman in a surprised tone, Ender turns to see a woman sitting on the museum floor. Ender replies Joseph should do nothing and that the woman will get up. He reminds Joseph they are late and need to leave.

Then the woman speaks up and says she has hurt her ankle. Ender looks down at the woman and sees she is sitting on her ankle. After telling Joseph to get her up and onto the bench, Ender watches the woman. Yes, it definitely appears she hurt her ankle. Ender's gaze moves up from the woman's ankle. Her legs are long and tanned underneath a pair of shorts that reach mid-thigh. The hips are narrow, and the waist is tiny, but what's above the waist catches Ender's eyes. The spaghetti-strapped tank top is stretched tightly over a generous bosom.

When Ender hears the woman ask if he will help, his eyes move up to her face, where he encounters dark brown eyes with flecks of amber. Naturally, the woman is angry, and the amber flecks ignite into fire.

The woman's anger is not only adding to Ender's frustration over being late, but also causing him to be angry. When he asks the woman if she knows who he is, she replies no and doesn't care. Everyone knows who I am, Ender thinks. I'm on the society pages of the newspaper almost daily. I have advertising posters all over the city. How can this woman not know me?

Ender reaches for his wallet, pulls out money, and offers it to the woman. He tells her to get a taxi and go to the doctor. When the woman refuses the money, calls him a pompous idiot, and Joseph snickers, Ender is almost at his breaking point. His face turns red with anger when he tells her to take the money. He is busy and doesn't have time to argue with her. The amber flecks flash in the woman's eyes. Ender cannot stop watching the flecks as they grow larger and brighter.

The woman tells him she's not from Istanbul and doesn't know where to find a doctor. When Ender asks her what she wants him to do, the woman replies with another smart remark about him being important enough to know a doctor and take her there.

By now, Ender realizes he will not win any argument with this angry woman, so he concedes. He sends Joseph to tell Azra, Ender's girlfriend, that he's delayed and will call her later. Azra will be furious, but this woman is so angry and in pain that Ender has no choice but to do something. What if the newspapers find out about the incident? They may report him as uncaring, leaving a woman in distress. That would ruin his public image, and since his image is so important to him, Ender cannot risk it.

After Burak leaves to get the car, Ender kneels in front of the woman. "Let me see your ankle," he demands. The woman lifts her leg, and Ender runs his hands over the delicate ankle. "Can you move it?" The woman moves it slightly. "Well, it doesn't appear to be broken. Let's get you to a doctor." Ender helps the woman stand, and she drops her purse on the floor. She bends to pick it up, and Ender's eyes go directly to her cleavage.

As the woman stands, she notices his eyes on her chest. "Did you get your eyes full?" the woman asks with a hint of amusement in her voice.

"I did and thought it was very nice," Ender replies with no emotion, looking into the brown eyes where the amber flecks have dimmed considerably. The woman rolls her eyes as Ender takes her arm, and the pair moves to the door where Burak waits with the car.

Ender helps the woman into the back seat, and he climbs into the front so the woman can rest her ankle on the seat. After a short, quiet drive, the three people arrive at Ender's private physician's home. The doctor quickly gives the woman an injection for the pain. Then, he determines the ankle is sprained and puts a brace on it.

"Ender, the injection will make her sleepy for several hours, and she shouldn't be alone. Who is with her, and where is she staying?" the doctor asks.

"I know nothing about her," Ender answers, watching the woman's eyes grow heavier and heavier. "Joseph knocked her down, and she fell on her ankle. She was so rude to me I didn't ask questions."

"Rude to you? I bet that was hard to take?" the doctor says, grinning. "Well, I looked at her passport, which is the only document she has with her. She's visiting from the US."

"I figured out she was American by her sarcastic attitude." Ender rubs his beard. "What do you suggest I do?"

"Take her to your place and let her sleep off the injection. Then you can find out where she's staying and take her there tomorrow," the doctor replies.

"You're kidding, right? I can't take her to my place. Azra will be even madder than she is now. Besides, the house is being remodeled, and my bedroom is the only usable one. What if the newspapers find out I took a stranger to my home?"

The doctor shakes his head in exasperation. "Ender, your ego and reputation will be the end of you. If the papers get the information, it will look like you helped an innocent American tourist injured in a fall. Now, take her to your house. Here are some painkillers for her. I suggest you avoid upsetting her more than she already is."

"What about how upset I am and Azra will be?" Ender asks.

"You'll get past it quickly. Azra might not, but she's not the right woman for you anyway," the doctor replies.

With no choice and the woman sleeping soundly, Ender picks her up and carries her to the car. He's not gentle when he places her in the back seat and climbs in himself. Ender props her against the opposite door and fumes. This woman has ruined his day, the party he was to attend, and probably his relationship with Azra. When Burak swerves to dodge a vehicle that pulls in front of the car, the woman's body falls over. Her head hits Ender's shoulder. He reaches to push her away, but he inhales the delicate fragrance of the woman. The scent is so different from the scents of Azra and other women he's known. It is light and sweet and unrecognizable. He inhales it deeply, as if committing it to memory.

When they arrive at the house, Ender lifts the woman and carries her to his bedroom. Funny, he thinks, I didn't notice how tiny she is before. Ender lays her down on the bed and starts to move away, but then he sits beside her and really looks at her for the first time. Between his anger and frustration, he hadn't taken the time to look at the woman except for her chest area. So now he starts at the top of her head.

The woman has dark brown hair with scattered golden highlights. Her hair is pulled back into a ponytail, so Ender estimates her hair is a little longer than shoulder length. She has long and dark eyelashes. Her cheekbones are high, her nose is perfect, and her lips are deep pink in the shape of a perfect cupid's bow. Ender reaches out and brushes his hand along her cheek, admiring the silky feeling of her skin.

All Ender's life, he has been drawn to beautiful women, always with perfect makeup. His ex-wife and girlfriends were all beautiful, but this woman was the most beautiful he had ever seen. The woman isn't wearing any makeup but doesn't need to. Her beauty is natural. Suddenly, Ender's phone rings, and he removes it from his pocket. It is Azra, so he lets it go to voicemail. The phone didn't disturb the woman because she didn't move at all. Ender takes a deep breath, knowing he needs to talk to Azra sooner rather than later. He stands, looks down at the woman, and leans over, kissing her perfect lips softly before leaving the room.

Once in the living room, Ender listens to Azra's ranting on the voicemail. All Azra does is nag, complain, and gossip these days. Maybe it's time to cut her loose, he thinks. I have already invited her to be my date next week for the annual gala. Perhaps I'll break up with her after that.

Ender calls Azra and explains why he missed the engagement party. He, however, leaves out the part about bringing the woman back to his house. When Azra insists on coming over, Ender makes the excuse that the remodeling has the house turned upside down. It is causing him to sleep on the sofa tonight. Then, Azra invites him to her apartment, but Ender says he is exhausted and going to bed. After telling Azra goodnight, he returns to his bedroom and pulls a chair next to the bed, where he can watch the woman sleep.

Chapter 3

Valerie

Valerie wakes the following morning and finds the man who took her to the doctor asleep in a chair beside the bed. She reaches over and wakes him.

"Where am I?" Valerie asks.

Hard Eyes rubs his eyes and replies, "at my house. I didn't know where you were staying, so I did not know what to do with you. The doctor said you sprained your ankle and couldn't be alone since he gave you the pain injection."

"Oh, okay. That makes sense. I better call a taxi and get to my hotel."

"I'll have Joseph take you. Here is a bottle of painkillers from the doctor. I know the label is in Turkish, but he said to take them as needed." Hard Eyes stands up and stretches. Valerie watches, noticing the broad shoulders and rippling muscles through the white dress shirt. His sleeves are rolled up to the elbow, exhibiting muscular, tanned forearms. Valerie's eyes travel downward to the tapered waist and lower to the hips where Hard Eyes' black slacks sit. Finally, her eyes travel back to the hard hazel eyes watching her.

"Thank you for taking care of me. I better go now." Valerie climbs off the bed, refusing to show she's in pain. Hard Eyes leads her to the living room while he taps on his phone. Seconds later, Joseph appears to take Valerie to her hotel.

Other than telling Joseph the name of her hotel, neither she nor Joseph speaks all the way across town. Finally, reaching the hotel, Valerie thanks the driver and heads up to her room to shower, take a painkiller, and lie down.

Valerie's ankle bothers her too much to visit any more sights in Istanbul her last two days, which disappoints her greatly. Valerie vows to return someday as she gets on the plane home. She will have to save a long time for the trip. At least she is returning to her job with a nice promotion, so perhaps she won't have to wait five more years before she can travel back.

Chapter 4

Valerie

Two years, three promotions, and five boyfriends later, Valerie sits at a sidewalk table eating her chicken salad sandwich. The day is unusually mild for Miami but humid, so she removes her suit jacket. That is so much better, she thinks, enjoying the ocean breeze on her shoulders and arm. Now, if only the day had started better than it did.

First thing this morning, all the senior management of the construction firm was called into a meeting. Two hours later, Valerie's boss informed her they had sold the firm. Just my luck, Valerie told him. I finally got my dream job, and now I have to look for another one. Her boss told her to wait and see what happened, but Valerie wasn't one to wait around. She has bills to pay and almost has enough saved to return to Istanbul. So Valerie immediately requested an extended lunch hour to search various websites for a new job. Starting over wouldn't be so bad, but she would have to work at least another year before being eligible for vacation time.

Valerie is deep in thought when she hears a voice ask, how's your ankle? She looks up at a man pulling the chair next to her away from the table. He quickly sits down, folds his hands on the table, and looks at her.

"I didn't ask you to join me," Valerie states, looking into the man's eyes. Oh my, I would know those eyes anywhere. It is the man from Istanbul.

"I know you didn't, but I asked you a question," the man replies sternly.

Already angry about the possibility of having to look for another job, Valerie looks directly at the hard eyes. "You should fire your doctor."

Hard Eyes is surprised and doesn't respond for several seconds. Then he says, "why?"

"Because my ankle was broken in two places and required surgery when I got back." Valerie slides her chair back and shows hard eyes the scars from her surgery. "I can make the alarms go off whenever I go through security. I have to carry several documents detailing my surgery and the hardware in my ankle."

"I suppose you would like me to apologize."

"No, I wouldn't expect a busy, important man like yourself to apologize for anything. What are you doing in Miami anyway, not that I care?"

"I'm here on business."

"Well, good for you," Valerie says, shoving her plate away so hard it almost slides off the table. She then puts her jacket on. "I wish I could say it's been nice seeing you again, but that would be a lie." She stands and walks off, feeling the man watching her every step.

Chapter 5

Ender

The meeting with the Miami city councilman went very well, Ender reflects. *I don't know why he sat at a sidewalk table in this humidity. My shirt is sticking to me, and I feel like a drowned rat.* Ender stands up as Joseph walks up.

"Sir, I know this sounds crazy, but do you remember the American woman I bumped into in Istanbul? She hurt her leg, and you took her to your doctor."

"Vaguely. Why do you ask Joseph?"

"Because she is sitting two tables behind you," Joseph answers.

"Are you sure it's her?"

"Of course I do. Isn't that what you pay me for?"

Ender turns around and looks at the woman. He can't be sure from the back, but there's only one way to find out. He walks over to the table. Next, he pulls out a chair next to her and sits down. "How's your ankle?"

When the woman looks at him and says she didn't ask him to join her, Ender knows it's her. The amber sparks ignite in her angry eyes, and he catches a whiff of the fragrance he hadn't forgotten. Next, she tells him he should fire his doctor, which catches him off guard. When Ender asks the woman why. She shows him an ankle with wide scars. She explains her ankle was broken, and she had to have surgery on it when she returned home.

Then the woman surprises him again when he says she probably expects an apology from him. She remembers Ender's words about being a busy, important man and says she doesn't expect an apology from a man like him. However, when she asks why he's in Miami, he replies on business and gets a typical sarcastic response from her. Next, she nearly pushed her plate off the table. Then, she got up and left with the ocean breeze catching her fragrance and blowing it right into his face.

Ender inhales deeply and looks down at the table. He rubs his forehead, remembering he spent months trying to find out what the fragrance was. Finally, Ender and a woman whose name he can't remember visited a botanical garden in Istanbul. It was there he found out it was jasmine. Ender vowed to himself if he ever saw the woman again, he would know her by the smell of jasmine and the amber sparks that explode from her angry eyes. Out of all the women in the world and all the places Ender had visited in the past two years, he finally came into contact with her again. Closing his eyes, Ender can still picture her lying on his bed and him bending down to kiss her perfect lips.

He would be kinder to the woman if he ever saw her again, Ender decided, or as kind as he was to any of the other women in his life, which wasn't very kind. Ender showered them with expensive gifts and trips, knowing they expected that. However, the women were dull and always demanding more, including his ex-wife. But something about this woman brought out his hard-as-nails attitude, no matter his intentions. Oh well, I'll probably never see her again anyway, he decides.

Ender stands, as does Joseph, and they make their way to the condominium Ender bought last month. The decorators finished his penthouse the previous week. Joseph and Matthew, the American bodyguard, live in a separate suite in the penthouse where they can monitor security. Ender quickly tours the floor below the penthouse, where the decorators assure him they will finish this week. The floor contains six apartments. Ender's housekeeper/cook will be in one apartment and his assistant in another. That leaves four vacant apartments available for future staff. Guests could also stay in the apartments if the three additional bedrooms in the penthouse are occupied.

After the tour, Ender goes to his office to work reading the personnel files of the people working for the company he just purchased. Tomorrow, he will begin interviewing the employees to decide who he will keep on and who will be let go. The plans for the severance packages have been developed, so Ender decides there is no reason not to move forward.

Chapter 6

Ender

It has taken Ender a week to interview everyone in a supervisory position in his new business. It didn't take long for him to decide the firm was top-heavy. Also, no one had the qualifications he needs to build his new hotel in Miami. However, Ender's architect in Turkey had completed the plans and would fly in next week to help hire construction personnel. Meanwhile, Ender was left to focus on the firm's remaining employees.

"Mr. Dogan, your next appointment, Ms. Valerie Richards, is here."

"Ms. Johnson, please give me five minutes and then send her in," Ender replies.

"Yes, sir."

Ender pulls Ms. Richards' personnel file from the stack on his desk and opens it. She has been with the firm for five years and has received three promotions in the past two years. In addition, they have highly ranked her in all her performance reviews, and she has several letters of commendation in the file. Ms. Richards has an undergraduate degree in Project Management from Arizona State University and an MBA from the University of Miami, which she completed during her time with the company.

There's a knock on the door, and Ender turns his back to the door, still reviewing the file. "Please come in and have a seat," he says to Ms. Richards. I'll be with you in a moment. He hears her take a seat and waits for a few seconds. "Ms. Richards, your personnel file is very impressive. Everyone that I've spoken to holds you in high regard."

Then Ender turns around to face Ms. Richards. They both say "YOU!" at the same time. Several seconds pass while each appears to be sizing the other up. Then, Ms. Richards gets up. "Where are you going, Ms. Richards?" Ender asks.

"I'm returning to my desk to pack my stuff. I'll be gone in an hour," Valerie says.

"Ms. Richards, please sit down. We haven't started the interview yet?"

"Really? Now that you know I'm Valerie Richards, do you still want to interview me?"

"Yes, actually, I do. Please," Ender says, motioning to the chair Valerie just left. Wow, he thinks, watching her walk slowly to the chair. She is dressed in a navy suit with a light blue blouse. The skirt hits Valerie above the knees, and she is wearing three-inch heels. Her shoulder-length hair frames her face, highlighting her brown eyes and pink cupid bow lips.

Once Valerie is seated, Ender walks around his desk and sits on the corner closest to her. The amber flecks in her eyes aren't visible to him, but the subtle fragrance of jasmine hits his nose. There it is, Ender thinks. It's really her.

"Ms. Richards, shall we begin?" Valerie nods. Ender goes through the typical interview questions. What are your goals, where do you see yourself in five years, etc.? Then he moves on to the firm and its future. Ender tells her of his plan to build a hotel in Miami and some challenges he's encountered since he's from Turkey. He talks about the different buildings he's built in Turkey. Then, he tells her why he wants to work in the US. Valerie listens intently and asks excellent questions along the way, which pleases Ender.

"Now, Ms. Richards, let's talk about you. I have a job in mind for you that differs from what you've done in the past. I haven't completed the job yet. I plan to work on it tonight and meet with you tomorrow to discuss it. Would you be interested, or shall I let you go pack up your office?"

"Mr. Dogan, I would be very interested in hearing your proposal."

"Good. Now check with Ms. Johnson to see what times I have available tomorrow. That is all for now." Ender watches as Valerie gets up and moves to the door. "Oh, Ms. Richards, would you ask Ms. Johnson to hold my next appointment for ten minutes before sending them in?" Valerie nods and leaves.

Ender stares at the door. What job? I haven't thought about a new position for anyone. I just promised to talk to Ms. Richards about a job tomorrow. Good gosh, what am I doing? It must be the jasmine. I wonder if it is hypnotic.

"Excuse me, Mr. Dogan," Ms. Johnson says over the intercom. "You have no free time tomorrow to meet with Ms. Richards."

"Is Ms. Richards available for dinner or at my home later in the evening?"

"No, sir. Ms. Richards says she has plans tomorrow night."

"Can she cancel her plans?" Ender asks. "After all, this is her future we are talking about?"

He hears Ms. Johnson talking to Ms. Richards. "Sir, Ms. Richards refuses to cancel her plans for tomorrow night."

Chuckling, Ender can picture Ms. Richards in front of Ms. Johnson's desk with her hands on her slim hips and the amber flecks flashing. "Well, tell Ms. Richards that I will be in touch." Ender pushes the button to end the call and turns to look out the window. "What am I getting myself into?" he says aloud.

Ender continues the interviews for the rest of the day, but his mind is on creating a new job for Ms. Richards. He is thinking about it during dinner with his assistant, Andrew.

"Mr. Dogan," Andrew begins. "I'm sorry to bring this up now because I know you have a lot on your mind, but I need help. I'm drowning between taking care of things in Turkey and here."

"Okay, Andrew. What would you like help with?" Ender asks. Andrew has been with Ender for ten years and has never complained about the workload or the hours. But Andrew is right. Ender is expecting him to take care of two very different Ender Dogan lives now.

"Well, you know I enjoy the business-related issues, and you, of course. But, if I had to choose one thing to give up that would help me, it would be your social life. It is almost as complicated as your business life."

"I agree my social life can get complicated and only worsen now that we're here. So let me think about it."

"Thanks, Mr. Dogan. Now, are you ready to talk about tomorrow?" Ender nods, and they spend the next hour discussing the following day.

Tired and frustrated, it doesn't take Ender long to fall asleep, but he dreams of Ms. Richards. She is beautiful, well-spoken, educated, has great style and taste in clothes, and can be a pain in the butt. So when the alarm goes off, Ender does something he rarely does. He lies in bed and thinks about his dream. Suddenly the solution to Andrew's problem and the new job Ender has to create is right before his eyes. He'll offer Ms. Richards the position of assistant in charge of his social life.

Ender jumps into the shower and begins making plans for the new position. First, he will have to make it very attractive to get Ms. Richards on board, but money talks.

Chapter 7

Valerie

Valerie looks in the mirror to apply her makeup for the day. It's going to be hard hiding these dark circles under my eyes, she determines. That's what I get for not sleeping. Between Hard Eyes, AKA Mr. Ender Dogan, and my date with Vince tonight, I'm a total wreck.

She thinks back to the meeting with Mr. Dogan. When she first sat down and only saw his back, Valerie had time to study the broad shoulders underneath that black fitted suit. I wonder what that man would look like naked, she thought. Then, when Mr. Dogan turned around, Valerie almost had heart failure when he turned out to be Hard Eyes from Turkey. He was pleasant, although he maintained those hard eyes the entire time she was in his office.

The possibility of a job unlike anything she had ever done was intriguing. But when Mr. Dogan had no time to meet today except for dinner or afterward at his home, Valerie had to say no. He was a stranger and could be her boss. She couldn't meet Mr. Dogan under those circumstances. Besides, she already had plans with Vince.

Valerie and Vince had been dating for six months and had recently talked about moving in together. I know that's what Vince wants to talk about tonight. I can feel it in my bones. So I'll suggest moving into his place. It is so much larger than mine, and we can have parties and invite our friends.

After dressing for work, Valerie lays out her red sundress and heels she intends to wear tonight for her date. She and Vince are meeting at Antonio's

Bar at 6:30, so she'll barely have enough time to change and walk the two blocks to the bar when she returns home from work.

Valerie walks into the bar at precisely 6:30. Vince waves at her from a table at the back. Vince doesn't hug or kiss Valerie like he usually does. It's a little confusing, but she brushes it off. The couple talks about their day over a drink. Then, out of the blue, Vince announces he is breaking up with Valerie. He tells her he's found someone else he'd rather be with. Shocked, Valerie can only sit and gawk at him. Vince tells her goodbye and walks out of the bar. Valerie tries not to cry, but a few tears escape her eyes. Thank goodness, I'm at a table in the back, she thinks.

"Can I buy you a drink?" a voice whispers so close to Valerie's ear that it sends shivers down her spine.

"No, thanks. I've had a rough night, and I'm not very good company," Valerie says, looking up into familiar hazel eyes.

Mr. Dogan gently wipes the tears from her cheeks and sits down next to Valerie. "I can see the evening didn't end as you had planned," he says softly.

"Are you following me, Mr. Dogan?"

"Yes, as a matter of fact, I am, or rather Joseph did, and he told me you were here."

"What do you want?"

"I want to talk about the job I want to offer you."

Valerie looks into his eyes and sees a totally unexpected softness. It only lasts for a few seconds, and then it's gone. "Okay, talk," she says.

"I have a personal assistant who is becoming overwhelmed between taking care of things here and in Turkey. He is a valuable employee who's been with me for ten years, and I don't want to lose him. So the job I'm offering you is to be a personal assistant to me, taking care of my social calendar."

"With all due respect, Mr. Dogan, I don't know anything about managing a social calendar," Valerie says.

"I know, but with your experience managing projects, I think you'll be very good at it."

"I know you're a busy, important man," Valerie smiles.

"And you know how to interrupt my social events," Mr. Dogan smiles back.

"You're an extremely handsome man when you smile."

"Ms. Richards, are you flirting with me?"

"No, sir. I would never presume to do such a thing. It was merely an observation."

"Well, thank you. I guess. Now let me tell you about the job and what I expect. I get invited to many social events. You and I would meet in the evenings to discuss which I want to attend. Next, you would either accept or decline on my behalf. This is for here and in Turkey. I expect you to learn the Turkish language to speak and read it. I can always find someone to write it, but it would be fine if you want to learn that too. Just like Andrew, you will travel with me wherever I go. You may be required to attend events with me at times. You will be available to me in person or by phone most of the time."

Valerie looks down at the table. "Don't you have a wife or girlfriend to take care of that for you?"

"No, Ms. Richards. I do not. I have an ex-wife who is getting married in two weeks, thank heavens. That means a trip to Turkey to celebrate her wedding and my financial freedom from that viper."

"When would you expect me to start if I took the job?"

"As soon as possible," Ender replies and studies Valerie's down-turned face for a few minutes. Then, finally, Valerie looks up at him. "Ms. Richards, you haven't asked me what's in it for you?"

"Why me, Mr. Dogan?"

"Ms. Richards, you intrigue me. I am surrounded by people who never ask questions or have an opinion. They certainly don't talk back to me. I appreciate your honesty, your temper, and your smart mouth." Ender says with a huge smile, showing his perfect teeth. "Now, what's in it for you? Well, to start, you would live in a furnished apartment one floor below me, here in Miami. In Turkey, you would have a suite inside my home. I will furnish all clothing, medical and dental expenses, travel expenses, and anything else I choose."

"Clothing?"

"Yes, I expect you to be dressed in a manner suited to you. As I said, you may be expected to attend events with me, so you would need attire for that. In addition, you will have clothing here, and in Turkey, so you wouldn't have to pack when we need to leave on short notice."

"What about free time?" Valerie asks.

"You will have free time to do as you wish. I will be very flexible if you have appointments or plans. You will have a driver to take you wherever you need to go. Your safety is a top priority for me. Regarding salary, I know I can be very demanding, so I'm prepared to offer you double what you are currently making."

"Mr. Dogan, that's way too much, especially if you're furnishing a place to live and clothing."

"Ms. Richards, I really want you to take this job. The salary is fair, considering what I will expect from you."

Valerie drops her head as if in thought for a few seconds, and her hair falls over her face. Ender watches her and then reaches out, tucking one side of her hair over her shoulder. His fingers softly brush Valerie's cheek. As she lifts her head, her eyes meet his. "Can I think about it?"

"Of course, Valerie," Ender whispers. "Today is Friday. I want an answer on Monday. Here is my card if you think of questions you wish to ask."

"Okay. This has been a long day for me, and you've given me a lot to think about. I'm going home."

"Can I give you a ride home?"

"No, thanks. I only live two blocks away."

"Will you let me walk you home, then? I told you safety is very important to me." Valerie shakes her head. "Good night, Mr. Dogan." She stands and walks toward the exit, feeling Mr. Dogan watching her all the way.

After leaving the bar, Valerie feels the hair on the back of her neck stand up. She turns around quickly and spots Joseph following her at a distance. She raises her hand and waves at him. He smiles, shrugs, and continues to follow her. After walking a block, Valerie sits on a bench and sobs, remembering Vince broke up with her. She feels something touch her shoulder and reaches up to swat it away. Instead of a bug, Valerie quickly realizes it is a handkerchief offered by Joseph. She takes it and continues to cry for several minutes before getting up and walking the rest of the way home.

Chapter 8

Ender

After signaling Joseph to follow Ms. Richards home, Ender sits at the table and contemplates everything he just offered her. Holy cow, I practically offered her the world on a silver platter. I didn't plan to provide that much, but the words just kept flowing out of my mouth on their own. She even told him it was too much. When I first wiped her tears away, I knew I had to have her close by me. Then, when I brushed her soft cheek as I moved her hair, I knew she was different. I may regret this one day, and I'm sure she will drive me crazy, but I need her with me, whatever that means.

As Joesph sits down at the table, Ender looks over at him. "That took longer than I expected. I thought she said she lived two blocks away."

"She does, but she had to stop about halfway and cry. Did you make her cry, Ender?"

"No, I think her boyfriend broke up with her tonight. That may work to my advantage."

"Ender, why is it so important that this woman comes to work for you?"

"I honestly don't know, Joseph. I just know I need her around me."

"Well, she made you smile tonight. I can't remember the last time you smiled."

Ender rolls his eyes at the comment. "Come on, Joseph. Let's go home."

"Yes, Mr. Dogan. I'll get the car."

That night, Ender dreams of a woman in a red sundress whose smile from pink cupid bow lips could light up a moonless night. Her brown hair is draped over the creamy skin of her shoulders. She is walking toward him in a meadow full of jasmine plants. As she nears, her smile turns into a frown, and tears fall from her eyes. Then the amber flecks from her eyes flash. I warned you never to talk down to me, the woman says. Suddenly, she turns and runs away from Ender as he calls for her to return. But the woman doesn't stop. Ender tries to follow her, but his feet are stuck in the mud, and he can't move. He calls the woman until she is no longer in sight. Then Ender falls to his knees and cries.

Ender wakes the following day covered in sweat. His sheets are wet, as is his pillow. He sits up and runs his fingers through his hair as he thinks about the dream. Everything about the woman in the dream reminded him of Valerie, but all he could see of the face were the eyes and the mouth.

Chapter 9

Valerie

After crying herself to sleep, Valerie sleeps in Saturday morning. She finally crawls out of bed at 10:00 am. After pouring a cup of coffee, she sits on the sofa and looks around the room. That was an interesting proposal Mr. Dogan made last night. I have no reason not to take the job because nothing ties me to Miami. My parents are gone, and now so is Vince.

So what are the pros of taking the job, Valerie asks herself? A rent-free apartment, clothes, travel, a driver, a job that doesn't sound highly complicated, and an excellent salary and benefits are seriously worth considering. What are the cons? I would have to give up my apartment and car, put my stuff in storage, be available to Mr. Dogan at all times, and work for an arrogant yet wealthy man.

Valerie reaches for her purse and pulls out the business card Mr. Dogan gave her last night. She stares at the card for several minutes and then dials the number on the card.

"Ender Dogan's office. This is Andrew. How may I assist you?" the voice on the other end of the phone says.

"Uh, Andrew. I'm sorry, I was expecting Mr. Dogan to answer the phone," Valerie replies.

"I am his assistant. What can I help you with today?"

"This is Valerie Richards. I wanted to ask Mr. Dogan a question."

"Ah, Ms. Richards. Mr. Dogan said you might call. I answer his phone on the weekends so he can have relaxation time. I can pass the question along if you like."

"Okay, well, I was wondering if I could see the apartment this weekend?"

"Of course, Ms. Richards. Would this afternoon at 2:00 pm work for you? I will be happy to show it to you," Andrew answers.

"This afternoon would be perfect. Would you text me the address?"

"Great. I'll send a driver to pick you up."

"That's unnecessary," Valerie says.

"Mr. Dogan would insist, Ms. Richards. Also, parking here would not be available. I'll have the driver pick you up at 1:45. Thank you for calling." Andrew hangs up without a goodbye.

"Well, okay then," Valerie says aloud. "1:45 it is." She showers and makes an early lunch. Since it is Saturday and she doesn't work for Mr. Dogan yet, Valerie dresses in shorts, a tank top, and sneakers. Then she waits on the sidewalk for the driver to appear. She is pleased to see Joseph when he gets out of the SUV and opens her door.

"Good afternoon, Ms. Richards."

"Hi. Do I call you Joseph?" The man nods. "Please call me Valerie."

"Yes, ma'am. I understand you want to see the apartment you might live in if you take the position with Mr. Dogan. I think you'll like it. The apartment is huge and tastefully furnished. Even though others are on the same floor, it is very private."

"I would have to put my things into storage, which concerns me a little," Valerie tells him.

"Here." Joseph reaches over the seat and hands Valerie a card. "This is my brother. He can help you with anything you need. If he can't, he can put you in touch with someone that can. So you keep his card with you at all times."

"That sounds a little ominous," Valerie says as she takes the card from him.

"Valerie, you are a brilliant woman, and I like you. You should know Mr. Dogan is a very demanding employer, but he has a good heart. He just doesn't show it often. He can be mean-spirited and has many resources available to him. He can always find people if he wants to."

"Joseph, that sounds like a warning."

"No, it's just the way things are. You may need options if you ever leave Mr. Dogan's employment. Just keep the card in a safe place. More importantly, you and I never had this conversation. Do you understand?"

"Okay, Joseph. Thank you." The rest of the ride is silent as Valerie ponders Joseph's words

Once they pull up to the curb of one of the tallest high-rise buildings in Miami, Joseph opens the door for her. Next, he gives her the elevator code to get to the eighty-fourth floor. "Andrew will let me know when you're finished, and I'll take you home. I hope you like the apartment," Joseph says.

"Hi! You must be Ms. Richards. Welcome!" A smiling man, approximately Valerie's age, greets her as the elevator doors open.

"And you must be Andrew," Valerie replies, shaking Andrew's offered hand. "Please call me Valerie."

"Great. Valerie, there are six apartments on this floor, and Mr. Dogan lives in the penthouse above," Andrew tells her as they walk down the hallway. "Currently, only the housekeeper and I live here. Mr. Dogan suggested you have the apartment that mirrors mine, so we both have the best views of Miami. So here we are," Andrew says, arriving at a door at the conclusion of the hallway. "I'm at the opposite end." He unlocks the door and pushes it open for Valerie. "I'll leave you alone to look at it. I'll leave my door open, so let me know when you're ready to leave."

Valerie thanks Andrew and steps into a vast living area with floor-to-ceiling windows to her right. In front of her is a small dining room, so she walks toward it. A modern kitchen with every appliance known to man is to her left. Valerie walks back into the living area and walks to the bedroom. Again, two walls are floor-to-ceiling windows. Next, she goes into the ensuite containing the closet and bathroom. The area is as large as the bedroom, but the bathtub catches her attention. It is large enough for two people. Valerie goes back into the bedroom and stands looking out at Miami.

"Do you like it?" a deep voice asks, catching Valerie off guard, and she jumps. "I'm sorry. I didn't intend to scare you."

"Mr. Dogan, I didn't expect to see you."

"Well, I expected to see you at some point this weekend," Mr. Dogan says, walking over to stand beside her. "This view is amazing, isn't it, Ms. Richards?" Valerie nods. "Over there is our office building." He points to Valerie's left. "Do you see it?"

"No, I don't."

"Here, let me show you," Mr. Dogan says, moving behind her and placing his hands on Valerie's shoulders. The gesture takes her by surprise, but even more surprising is the warmth of his touch on her shoulders. His hands are firm but gentle. When he lifts his right hand to point in the building's direction, Valerie feels his breath against her ear. It sends shivers throughout her body. "Can you see it now?" he asks.

It takes a few seconds for Valerie to respond to Ms. Dogan's question because she is taken aback by her body's reaction to his touch. "No, not yet," Valerie finally answers.

"Let me see if I can help. Do you see the tall blue building?"

"Yes."

"It is two buildings to the left of the blue building." Mr. Dogan's breath tickles Valerie's ear.

"Okay, now I do. Thanks," Valerie replies, stepping away, forcing him to remove his hands from her shoulders. "The apartment is beautiful."

"I thought you might like the colors. Although it is furnished, you are welcome to bring anything with you. Since you asked to see the apartment, does this mean you are considering my proposal?"

Valerie looks into the hard hazel eyes and briefly sees the hardness disappear. It happens so fast that she wonders if it is her imagination. "Yes, I'm considering it, but I will have a few stipulations."

Mr. Dogan smiles broadly, making Valerie's heart skip a beat. "I would have been disappointed if you didn't." He turns away from her and looks out the windows again.

Valerie observes Mr. Dogan. He is wearing a white short-sleeved polo shirt showing off his tanned, muscular forearms. The shirt is tight across broad shoulders and is tucked into the waistband of fitted black jeans. Black sneakers without socks complete his outfit.

"Mr. Dogan."

"Yes, Ms. Richards?"

"Do you ever wear anything besides black and white?"

"Well, that's a question I would have never expected you to ask," Mr. Dogan says without turning around. "In my world, black and white signify strength and professionalism. So why do you ask?"

"I think you need a little color in your life. Black and white are boring. Oh, and I suggest losing the vest. I know it is professional, but you'll be a hot mess here in Miami."

"I will take your suggestions under consideration, Ms. Richards. Now, I need to leave you unless you have questions, comments, or suggestions," Mr. Dogan says, turning around to face Valerie. The hard eyes are back.

"No, I've seen enough. Thank you for taking time out of your busy day to visit with me. I'll go let Andrew know I'm ready to leave." Mr. Dogan nods and walks out of the room and the apartment.

After Joseph drops Valerie off at her apartment, she walks through each room. She tries to determine what items she would put in storage and which she would take with her if she took the job. Later, while eating a frozen dinner, Valerie thinks about her body's response to Mr. Dogan's warm breath on her ear. Finally, she decides that nothing good would come out of any thoughts or ideas about him.

Chapter 10

Ender

"Well, that was a pleasant surprise," Ender says aloud as he rides the elevator up one floor to his penthouse. "I expected her tomorrow, not today." When he enters his apartment, he goes directly to the windows and looks over Miami. He thinks I shouldn't have touched her, but the fragrance of jasmine was too overpowering. Her skin was so soft when I touched her shoulders.

"Ender, are you coming back to bed?" a woman asks loudly. "I'm lonesome and miss your touch."

"Yes, Melissa. I'll be there in a few minutes." Melissa. At least the high-priced whores in Miami have typical names, unlike those that walk the streets. Ender looks out the window for several more minutes, wondering if the job he offered Valerie Richards is enticing enough for her to take it. Maybe I need to devise one or two more incentives to ensure she can't resist. I'll contemplate that after Melissa leaves later. After all, I booked her all day, and she hasn't disappointed me.

Pulling his shirt over his head as he enters his bedroom, Ender stops to gaze at the naked woman in his bed. She is beautiful but full of silicone and Botox, unlike the natural beauty of Valerie Richards. He finishes dressing and climbs into bed next to Melissa. She pushes him onto his back, where he laces his hands together behind his head. Next, Melissa goes to work to satisfy Ender's desires. He closes his eyes and remembers Valerie's jasmine fragrance, brown eyes, and perfect lips.

The sun is setting, and Melissa is getting dressed. "Ender, my boss is having a party tonight at the club. Why don't you come with me? You'll have time to meet other women if I'm unavailable."

"No, thank you, Melissa. Unfortunately, I have some work to do."

"Oh, come on, Ender. Tomorrow is Sunday. You can work then. Besides, you can make some new business contacts there. You'd be surprised how many business executives like yourself enjoy the company of a beautiful woman or two or three," Melissa says with an enormous grin.

"I'll think about it." Ender picks up his phone and opens an app. "You really earned your money today. I think a $2,000 tip is in order."

"Thank you, Ender. That's very generous of you. Well, goodnight. You know how to find me if you get lonesome."

"I'll text Joseph. He'll meet you downstairs in the car. Goodnight, Melissa."

A party at the club. That sounds enticing, Ender thinks. He's met several vital connections at the club. First, the club caters to men like him that enjoy the company of beautiful, sophisticated women. It is about a 50-50 split between married versus single men. Nothing sexual happens at the club. Several bars are scattered throughout the club, with a members-only club on the floor above. If one chooses, anything that occurs between a man and a woman or women happens after leaving the club. Melissa's boss owns the club and only employs the best women. They are highly educated, well-mannered, and well-trained. Ender smiles at the well-trained thought. He's even used a couple of women as his date for social events.

But not tonight, Ender decides. He needs to concentrate on what additional items he can offer Valerie Richards to get her to take the job. As he eats dinner, Ender mentally reviews the list of things he's already offered. He offered a furnished apartment and a separate wing of his home in Istanbul. He included clothes, a driver, medical and dental, travel expenses, and free time. Her salary is so generous that she can never spend as long as she's in his employment. Hmmm, maybe I should add jewelry. No, she's not that type of woman, plus I can borrow any jewelry she might need. What about a car? No, she'll have a driver, and her safety is my concern. As soon as people find out she works for me, she may become a target. What about education? She's already got an MBA, and I told her I expected her to learn the Turkish language. Well, I have tomorrow to think about it. I'll reread her file, and maybe something will come to me.

It is still early, so Ender decides to go to the club. He changes and asks Joseph to bring the car around. Ender says on the way to the club, "Joseph, I'm concerned Ms. Richards may not take the job. I've offered her the moon. I'm trying to decide what else to add to sweeten the offer. Do you have any suggestions?"

"Ender, I don't get the impression that material things are significant to Ms. Richards. She seems like a gracious lady that should be treated as such. Remember that, Ender. She's a lady, not one of those women you meet at the club or takes to events or your ex-wife. You treat her like you do most of your employees, and she'll be gone quickly."

"Joseph, you make me sound horrible."

"Ender, I've known you a long time. I'm probably the only real friend you have. So I can talk to you honestly. You can be a mean SOB and treat people like dirt underneath your shoes. I'm just saying be careful with Ms. Richards. She's different from anyone you have ever known."

"I have to agree with you. She's different. I can't seem to get her out of my mind. Maybe once she is working for me, that will change."

Joseph looks in the rearview mirror and into Ender's eyes. "I don't think it will change. We're here. I'll be around the corner when you get ready to leave." Ender nods and gets out of the car.

It was 4:00 am by the time Ender got home from the club, so he sleeps until 11:00. He only woke up when his housekeeper came in twice to check on him.

Dressed and eating lunch, he thinks about Valerie Richards again and possible incentives. So far, he has come up empty. Ender goes to his office, retrieves her personnel file, and looks through it while eating.

Ms. Richards has no next of kin listed anywhere. Her emergency contact is the previous boss that she worked with for three years. I didn't intend to keep the guy on, but that might be the incentive I need. If Ms. Richards listed him as her next of kin, she must have a close relationship with him. I wonder how close. Well, I'll keep that as an option after I hear what she has to say. Ender devotes the rest of the day reading proposed employment contracts of the people he wants to keep hoping to hear from Ms. Richards, but she never contacts him.

Chapter 11

Valerie

Monday morning comes early for Valerie. After spending part of Sunday crying over the loss of Vince, she decided about Mr. Dogan's offer. She wants to get into the office early and meet with him if he's available.

Even though Valerie knows Mr. Dogan's assistant, Ms. Johnson, won't be in until 8:00 am, Valerie enters the reception area, hoping Mr. Dogan arrives at the office early as well. She knocks on his door and is surprised when she hears him say come in.

"Excuse me, Mr. Dogan. Do you have a few minutes to talk?"

"Of course, Ms. Richards. Please have a seat." Mr. Dogan gets out of his chair. "Would you like a cup of coffee?" Valerie nods. He gets two cups from the credenza behind his desk and carries one to her. Valerie watches the handsome man walking toward her. She notices his vest is missing and smiles. Next, he sits down in a chair beside Valerie, surprising her. "I hope you have good news for me," Mr. Dogan says with a smile.

"Mr. Dogan, I want to accept your offer, but as I said on Saturday, I have a few stipulations."

"I'm all ears, Ms. Richards."

"First, I require a week to get things in order. I need to plan for my car and apartment. Second, never criticize me in front of others. If you have a problem with me, please talk to me privately," Valerie says. "Third, never talk down to me. I am a human being. I deserve respect from you and others. I won't stay with you if you are ever condescending to me. Fourth, please call me Valerie."

"Okay, Valerie, unless in a professional setting. I'm sure you can understand that. Now, I want you to start today. However, I can understand having things to take care of. So, here's my thought. Do whatever you need to do during the day, and you can work in the evenings for me, beginning tonight. Will that work for you?" Mr. Dogan asks.

"Yes, sir, and thank you."

"Things are different here than in Turkey, and I understand that. I was educated here in the US and took several HR classes to learn how to treat people. Sometimes I lose my temper because I get frustrated. I will try my best to treat you with respect and professionalism at all times. Last, please call me Ender, except in a professional setting. Joseph will pick you up tomorrow at 9:00 am and take you to a nearby store. I will call the head of the store and tell them to expect you. I will also tell them what clothing and shoes you need. Tell your supervisor you will be late if you still need to come into the office."

"Thank you, Ender, for the opportunity to work for you."

"Valerie, I prefer to think of it as working with me. Dinner is at 7:00. We will work during dinner and afterward if needed. Andrew will join us. My housekeeper is a wonderful cook, so come hungry. Joseph will pick you up. I'll see you tonight." Knowing that was Ender's way of dismissing her, Valerie leaves the office and goes to her own to tell her boss of her plans.

After speaking to her boss, Valerie pulls out the card Joseph gave her. She calls Joseph's brother, and they agree to meet at her apartment at 2:00. Valerie gets to work on organizing everything because she doesn't plan to return to the firm after this morning.

"My brother told me you might call," the man says when Valerie opens her apartment door. "I'm Damon."

"Hi, Damon. Please come in. I'm Valerie. Thank you for meeting me on short notice, but I need help to get things done this week."

"That's what I'm here for. So let's sit down, and you tell me what you need."

Valerie explains she needs to rent a storage building. First, she needs to store her furniture and belongings, which she needs help packing. Next, she needs someone to move her things to the storage facility. Finally, she needs to sell her car.

Damon writes everything and asks a few questions. "I can take care of all of this for you. Can we get started tomorrow?"

"Tomorrow after lunch would be perfect. I'll pack the things I'll take with me later and be out of your way. I'm not sure how much longer I'll need the car, but I should have an answer for you tomorrow," Valerie says.

"Great. I'll see you tomorrow," Damon says.

"Oh, I guess I should ask you how much and if you take a check or prefer cash."

"We'll discuss that when my work is finished."

After Damon leaves, Valerie packs a few items, like family pictures, to take with her. Then she inventories her clothes. She'll better know what to pack after shopping for clothing tomorrow. When she looks at the clock, Valerie is stunned to see it is 6:00. Someone will probably pick her up between 6:30 and 6:45, so she quickly showers. Unsure what to expect, Valerie dresses in a green silk blouse and a black pencil skirt with three-inch heels. Finally, she stuffs a new daily planner she bought over the weekend into her tote, along with her laptop, several pens and pencils, and a notebook.

After picking her up, Joseph escorts Valerie to the penthouse, where they find Ender and Andrew relaxing on the sofa, both dressed in jeans and t-shirts.

"Valerie," Ender stands and smiles. "I apologize for not telling you to dress casually, but you look great. Andrew, we might start dressing for dinner."

"Not me," Andrew says. "You make me wear a suit all day, so my evenings are my time. Hi Valerie. Welcome to the team."

"Hi, both of you. Something smells amazing."

Ender nods. "Yes, it does. Would you like a glass of wine before dinner?"

"No, thank you. I want to have a clear head."

"Okay let's eat and get started."

Andrew starts by explaining the social calendar he has set up. He has already set Valerie up as an admin and shows her how to download the calendar. Next, Andrew explains he will access the calendar as well.

Ender tells Valerie he has already purchased a laptop and printer for her, and they are in her apartment. He explains she is to bring any invitations with her to their daily meetings. The two of them will discuss which ones he will attend. It will be Valerie's responsibility to either accept or decline each invitation. Ender will also tell Valerie if he plans to attend alone or with someone.

Next, the three discuss the events Ender has already agreed to attend and what he will wear. Valerie will ensure his clothing choices are cleaned and ready for him. Finally, they discuss Ender's return to Istanbul for his ex-wife's wedding on Tuesday. They will leave Miami on Saturday. Ender tells Valerie she will travel with him, shop for clothing while she is there, and get her suite in order.

After dinner, Ender gives Valerie all the codes to access the elevator for her floor and the penthouse. He also explains dinner is always at 7:00 sharp. That will be Ender's and Valerie's meeting time unless he notifies her otherwise. Then he excuses himself, leaving Andrew and Valerie to talk about things like laundry, housekeeping, food, etc.

It is 11:00 when Joseph drops Valerie off at her residence. She's exhausted and goes to bed, deciding to review the calendar tomorrow.

Chapter 12

Ender

nder can hardly keep his mind on today's business. Valerie agreed to work with him, and he's excited. He's never been this happy about a new employee, he realizes. Now, he will be close to this woman who puts him in his place daily. He's looking forward to dinner tonight and seeing her reaction to her new job duties.

After he calls the store's manager, they put Ender in touch with the department head for women's clothing. First, he explains the clothing he wants Valerie to have. There are no limitations on cost. Next, he gives the department head his credit card information. Next, Ender calls his credit card company and orders two cards for Valerie. One is his personal account, and the other is his business card. Ender requests the cards be delivered tomorrow before 5:00 pm.

Finally, Ender orders a laptop and printer to be delivered to Valerie's new apartment by the end of the day. He texts Joseph about the laptop and printer delivery. He also texts Joseph the time to pick Valerie up for dinner and to inform Andrew to pick him up from the office. Ender wants Joseph can stay at the penthouse waiting for the technology deliveries.

Finally, the workday ends. Ender hurries home to get in his workout, shower, and change before Valerie arrives. Andrew is waiting for him when Ender walks into the living area. They discuss how to introduce Valerie to Ender's social world.

When Valerie arrives wearing a black pencil skirt with a green blouse, Ender is overtaken by how gorgeous she looks dressed so simply. He wishes he had worn something besides a t-shirt and jeans. It pleases Ender when Valerie refuses a glass of wine, wanting to keep her head clear.

Throughout dinner and the discussion about Ender's social calendar, Valerie asks intelligent questions and takes many notes. Ender finds it hard to focus on his food instead of the beautiful woman sitting across from him. He watches her closely when she takes notes or asks Andrew questions. When she looks in his direction, Ender quickly averts his eyes.

After dinner, Ender gives Valerie the codes she needs for the building and then excuses himself to go to his office. I don't have any work to do, but I need to get away from Valerie. There's something about her that stirs unfamiliar feelings in me. I don't know what those feelings are, but I hope to figure it out soon. If she isn't suitable for the job or is untrustworthy, I need to know quickly.

Chapter 13

Valerie

Joseph picks Valerie up promptly at 9:00 am and drops her off at a store her bank account never allowed her to set foot in. She is greeted warmly by a woman a few years older than she is and taken to the women's department. The woman tells Valerie Mr. Dogan requested several specific outfits for her. The color choices are to be decided by Valerie and the head of the department.

It is noon when Valerie is ready to leave the store. All the clothing will be delivered to her new apartment. The clothing comprises new lingerie, five suits with skirts and pants, blouses for the suits, three cocktail dresses, and two evening gowns. There are even different shoes to match each outfit. In addition, Valerie is given a business card of the store's best stylist, that will come to the apartment and do Valerie's hair and makeup when needed.

When Joseph pulls up to the curb of Valerie's apartment, he laughs aloud. There are ten people, including his brother, waiting for Valerie. "Damon told you he would take care of things. Be ready. He's like a hurricane when he gets started." After opening the door for Valerie, Joseph talks briefly to his brother and then tells Valerie he will pick her up for dinner at 6:40.

Once inside the apartment, all the people pack the rooms for Valerie. She goes to her bedroom and selects which clothes to take with her. She chooses all her underwear, all her casual clothes and shoes, and three of her best suits and blouses. She packs those, setting the suitcases by the door along with the one box of possessions she decided to take with her. By then, it is 3:00, so

Valerie texts Joseph, asking if he could pick her up soon. He responds he will be there in twenty minutes.

Joseph arrives, and he loads Valerie's things into the SUV. Valerie gives Damon her key to the apartment and her car keys. Valerie wipes a few tears from her eyes as she leaves the place that has been home for five years. She looks up at the rearview mirror and receives a comforting smile from Joseph.

Valerie takes a deep breath and holds it for a few seconds when Joseph opens the door for her. She looks up at the high-rise building and can't believe she is actually going to live here and work for the handsome man with hard hazel eyes. Joseph tells Valerie he will bring her things up after he parks the SUV.

Valerie opens the door to the apartment and walks inside. She drops her tote on the sofa and looks around. Sitting on the island in the middle of the kitchen is the largest vase of yellow roses Valerie has ever seen. She thinks there must be at least three dozen roses, walking over to them.

Finding the card, Valerie opens it and reads, "Welcome to the world of a busy, important man, but most of all, welcome to my life." Valerie smiles and wonders if Ender will ever forget her sarcastically, calling him a busy, important man. She immediately texts him, thanking him for the flowers.

At 6:55, Valerie grabs her tote and heads upstairs for dinner. Ender is waiting for her at the elevator.

"Good evening, Valerie. Are you all moved in?"

"Yes, and thank you for everything, Ender."

"Dinner is ready. Shall we get started?" Valerie nods and follows him to the dining room.

"Ender, I assume these are the invitations that were received today. I found them on my table," Valerie says, holding several envelopes.

"They probably were. Andrew gets all the mail and then sorts it. Shall we go through them?"

There are five invitations, and Ender turns down four of them. The one he wants to accept is for an opening of an exclusive club downtown in four weeks. He tells Valerie to RSVP because they will return from Istanbul by then. Ender also tells her to respond that he will bring a guest. Next, they go through his social calendar for the rest of the week. Ender has a gala to attend Thursday night that will require a tuxedo. He tells her he will get it for her to take to the cleaners before she leaves tonight.

"Valerie, I know you said you needed to take care of things this week, but are you free tomorrow at lunch?"

"Actually, I finished everything today, so I'm all yours."

"Wonderful. My architect from Istanbul arrived today, and we are interviewing a project manager tomorrow. Unfortunately, no one in the firm meets my qualifications for the job I want to be done. I would like you to attend and provide me with your feedback on the woman. I'll send you the details in the morning," Ender says. "Valerie, you have eaten little. Was everything okay?"

"Ender, I'm allergic to shellfish and don't care for fish. Everything else was perfect."

"Can I get you something or have the housekeeper make something for you?"

"No, I'm fine. Thank you, though. Ender, I noticed you didn't wear your vest yesterday," Valerie smiles.

"I have to admit, you were right." Ender gives her a panty-dropping smile. "It is cooler without it. I also thought about what you said about always wearing black and white."

"Well, it looks a little intimidating and funeral-like."

Ender laughs aloud, which Valerie hears for the first time. It is a delightful laugh and makes her laugh. "I make a deal with you," he says. "When I get the tux, you can see at my suits. Then you can go shopping for shirts and ties. If I like them, I'll wear them. If not, you get the pleasure of returning them."

"That's a deal I'll gladly take. Now, if there's nothing else, I better go. You probably have work to do."

"I do, but will you have a glass of wine with me before you go? I wish to get to know you as a person," Ender says almost shyly.

"Okay. I'd enjoy that." Valerie packs up her tote as Ender gets their wine. Then the pair goes to the living area. Valerie sits down on the sofa, tucking one leg under her. Ender sits on the opposite end and turns to face her.

"So, Ender, what would you like to know?"

"Tell me about you. I know about your education and professional life. What about your personal life? I don't need to hear about your private life. Only share what you are comfortable with, and I'll share some of mine."

Valerie opens her mouth to talk, but at that moment, the elevator opens, and a boisterous man steps out with two beautiful women.

"Ender, look who I ran into at the club, your old friend, Melissa, and this is my new friend Sophia."

Valerie looks at Ender, who is staring at the three people. Then she looks at the woman named Melissa. The woman is beautiful, with a perfect body in a skintight dress. Valerie watches as the woman walks over to Ender and sits on his lap. "I need to go," Valerie says, standing.

"Who is this lovely creature?" the man asks.

Valerie looks at Ender, who caresses Melissa's knee while smiling. Since Ender is obviously preoccupied, Valerie answers, "just another employee." She grabs her tote and hurries into the elevator, which thankfully is still on Ender's floor.

Valerie realizes she forgot Ender's tux once inside the confines of her apartment. I'll just get it early in the morning and drop it off. She sits on the sofa, thinking about what she just witnessed. The man must be Ender's architect from Turkey because he had access to the penthouse. The women, however, were fascinating. Valerie had heard about the working women of Miami but had never seen one. Well, I sure saw two tonight, she thinks. What surprised her the most was Ender's familiarity with the one named Melissa. He is a man, and men have needs, just like women. Valerie smiles to herself and says aloud, "at least my needs are satisfied mechanically and a lot cheaper."

Chapter 14

Valerie

Valerie enters Ender's apartment at 9:00 with plans to grab a late breakfast and his tux. However, while the housekeeper is making Valerie's toast, she tells Valerie that Ender is not up yet, which surprises Valerie.

Starting on her second piece of toast, Valerie hears sounds behind her and turns around to see Ender wearing only a towel, kissing Melissa on the cheek. Ender tells Melissa he will pick her up at 7:00 pm for the gala. Then he presses the call button for the elevator. Once Melissa is on the elevator, Valerie turns around quickly. She turns the volume up on her earbuds and closes her eyes, trying to concentrate on the music rather than the vision of the handsome man wrapped in a towel.

Feeling something brushing her cheek, Valerie opens her eyes. She finds Ender looking at her while pushing a lock of her hair behind her ear. He pulls the earbud out and smiles.

"Good morning, Valerie. No wonder you didn't hear me the first time," he says, holding up her earbud.

"Ender, I came to get your tux that I couldn't get last night."

"Sorry about last night. I got distracted." He smiles and winks at her. "We can finish our conversation another time."

Valerie looks into Ender's eyes, knowing the amber flecks of anger are visible. "I'm sure your distraction was way more interesting than listening to me talk. Would you mind getting your tux for me so I can get going?"

Ender stares into Valerie's eyes and smirks. "If you come with me, you can look at my suits just as we talked about last night."

"No, thanks for the suits, but if you don't have the energy to get the tux, I will."

"I can assure you, Ms. Richards, I have a great deal of stamina," Ender says as his eyes bore holes into hers. Then he turns and goes toward his bedroom. Valerie can't help but watch. Muscles ripple as he walks from the top of Ender's shoulders to where the towel sits on his hips. The calves of his legs are muscular and tanned like his arms. Valerie inhales deeply, feeling a longing inside her.

When Ender returns with the tux, he wears pajama pants hanging very low on his hips. He strolls, seemingly to tempt Valerie, but she deliberately turns her back to him, looking at her phone. In reality, she has the phone in reverse camera mode and is filming Ender walking toward her.

"Here's my tux," Ender says as he lays it across Valerie's arm as if to block her phone purposely.

"Thanks. I'll have it back to you as soon as possible." Valerie stands, refusing to look at Ender, knowing her eyes would roam all over his body if she did. Instead, she hurries to the elevator and waits for it to arrive.

"See you tonight, Valerie," Ender says in a voice that some might say is sexy, but Valerie knows the cold hard eyes are anything but.

Fortunately for Valerie, the dry cleaner is half a block from the apartment building. It doesn't take her long to drop off the suit and return to her apartment. She plops down on the sofa and watches the video she took of Ender walking toward her. Wow, he is so hot, Valerie thinks. She enlarges the footage and can faintly see the blond hair covering his chest, then working its way down past his abs to the waistband of his pants. Ender smiles broadly, showing his perfect white teeth, but the cold hard eyes never soften.

Suddenly a text message appears from Joseph asking if she needs to go anywhere today. Valerie responds she needs to go to a food store after the lunch meeting. I need to buy food so I can avoid going to the penthouse as much as possible. Joseph replies he will be downstairs at 11:15 to pick her up and take her to the office for the lunch interview with the architect. Valerie looks at her phone. She has an hour to shower and dress.

All the clothes Ender bought for her arrived yesterday, so Valerie handpicks a navy suit with a red silk blouse that shows a little cleavage. Looking at herself in the mirror, Valerie smiles. This suit is so fitted. It looks like I painted it on. She chooses navy five-inch heels to wear. "I bet Melissa doesn't look this good in a suit," Valerie says aloud. "Why do I care how Melissa looks?" she asks the mirror and receives no answer.

"You look gorgeous today, Valerie," Joseph tells her as he opens the door.

"Joseph, I haven't decided if we can read each other's minds or if we have some type of ESP," Valerie laughs.

Joseph waits until he's inside the SUV and looks at Valerie in the rearview mirror. "I don't know, Valerie, but they say great minds think alike. Watch my body language if you don't know what I'm thinking." Valerie nods, not fully understanding, knowing that Joseph is warning her.

It's still a little early when Valerie arrives at the office, so she waits in the SUV with Joseph. They talk about general topics and are in the middle of a discussion about Miami politics when the door next to Valerie opens. The man from last night climbs into the back seat beside her. When Ender opens the opposite door and starts to get in, he looks at Valerie.

"Uh, Ender," Valerie says. "It's going to be crowded, so let me sit up front with Joseph."

"No way, Valerie." Ender gets in and sits next to her. "Valerie, this is Murat, my architect. Murat, this is Valerie, my new personal assistant."

"Ah, the beauty from last night. You left before I could introduce myself," Murat says with a chilling grin.

"Well, you were very preoccupied." Valerie notices Murat moves a little closer to her than is necessary. She looks into the rearview mirror to find

Joseph watching her. He shakes his head slightly, so Valerie moves closer to Ender. Ender glances at her with a confused look, but Valerie gives him a small smile.

The lunch interview went well, Valerie thinks, on the ride to the food store. Unfortunately, she was seated between Murat and Ender, and Murat always seemed to find a reason to touch her hand or arm, which made her uncomfortable.

"Joseph, how well do you know Murat?"

"I try to avoid him as much as possible," Joseph replies. "Did he bother you?"

Valerie ponders the question for a few seconds. "No, but he really makes me uncomfortable, and I don't know why."

"Trust your instincts, Valerie. Now, here we are. I'll wait for you here."

After returning from the food store, Valerie works all afternoon, replying to event invitations for the next two weeks that Ender will be in Istanbul. Finally, at 6:55, she heads up to the penthouse and finds Ender waiting at the elevator.

"Come, Valerie. We have a lot to discuss since we won't meet tomorrow night. I have asked the housekeeper to provide you with the dinner menu each week so you can let her know if you have any allergies or dislikes."

"That's very kind of you. Thanks," Valerie says, sitting down at the dining table. "You didn't receive any invitations today, and I declined all invitations for the two weeks you will be gone."

"Good. Since Andrew will be in Istanbul with us, Ms. Johnson will come by every day and gather the mail to send to me for overnight delivery while we are gone. Now, tell me your thoughts on the project manager interview today."

Ender listens carefully to Valerie's thoughts and asks questions as they go. He seems genuinely interested in my opinion, Valerie thinks as she pauses once to gather her thoughts. When she's finished, Ender tells her she has good intuition and observation skills.

"Valerie, if you're finished eating, why don't we go relax and talk?" Ender says.

"Thank you for dinner, but I have a few personal things to tend to before bed. If we aren't meeting tomorrow night, your housekeeper does not need to make dinner for me tomorrow night. I bought food today."

"I'll tell her, but she still cooks for Joseph and Andrew, so you are always welcome. Well, good night then," Ender says as Valerie walks to the elevator. "Oh, Valerie." She turns to look at him. "You looked stunning today. Was that one of the new suits I bought?"

He should have stopped at you looked stunning, Valerie thinks as her face turns pink with anger and the amber flecks shoot out of her eyes. "Yes, Mr. Dogan. It was one you so kindly purchased for me. I'm happy you were pleased." Valerie turns and stomps into the elevator.

Chapter 15

Ender

"What did I say wrong?" Ender says aloud, throwing up his hands in frustration.

"You shouldn't have asked if that was a suit you bought," Joseph says, walking into the room.

"Why not? I wanted to know."

"Two reasons, you stupid man. First, it totally erased the compliment you gave Valerie. Second, you never complimented her on her clothes, making her feel like they weren't good enough for you."

"How do you know so much about women, Joseph?"

"I grew up with six older sisters. I paid attention to what they said, did, and thought. Valerie won't say anything to you, but Murat makes her uncomfortable. That's why she sat closer to you in the car."

"Murat is Murat. He's a brilliant architect and fun to be around."

Joseph sits on the sofa and watches Ender pace in front of him. "And Melissa is fun to be around too?"

"Melissa is a pleasant woman and fun in her own way, even if she is expensive. So why are you bringing her up? Are you talking about Murat showing up with her last night?" Joseph nods. "I did not know Murat would bring her here."

"I know you didn't, but you sure didn't handle it very well. Two expensive whores and a lady. One whore walks in and sits on your lap, and you run your hand along her thigh."

"Well, she turns me on. So what's your point, Joseph?"

"How do you think seeing that made a lady like Valerie feel?"

"It doesn't matter how she felt. She's an employee, and my personal life is none of her business."

"Okay, but wasn't her attitude different after that? Think about that, Ender," Joseph says, walking out of the room.

Ender watches Joseph leave and runs his fingers over his chin. Joseph was right. Valerie's demeanor was different today. It was distant, and she got angry twice. Those amber flecks sparking from her eyes like fireworks on the 4th of July. It's my life, and I can live it. I will live it without worrying about what Valerie thinks.

Ender walks into his bedroom, finding his newly cleaned tux lying on the bed. He picks it up to put it in the closet and catches a whiff of jasmine. Ender inhales deeply and realizes he cares what Valerie's feelings are. He's never cared about a woman's feelings before, and why should he? But Valerie is different somehow and essential to his life. He just doesn't know why.

Chapter 16

Ender

It is 4:00 pm on Saturday, and everyone but Valerie is at the curb waiting on the limo to take them to the airport. Shortly, the car arrives, and everyone gets in, but still no Valerie. They wait for several minutes. Finally, Joseph gets out of the car and says he will go upstairs to get her.

"No, I'll go," Ender says. "She probably overslept. I don't need this problem with my headache and hangover." He stomps off to the door of the building.

He knocks hard on Valerie's door, and she quickly opens it, turning her back to him. "Why aren't you downstairs at the limo like everyone else?" Ender yells.

She turns around and looks directly into his eyes. The amber flecks turn into golden daggers flying at Ender rapidly, threatening to rip him to shreds. "How dare you ask me that, you busy, important man? You're so busy and important that you haven't been at work or home for two days. You have answered none of my texts or emails asking about travel plans. Andrew is already in Istanbul, so that I couldn't ask him. Ms. Johnson did not know the plans or how to get in touch with you," Valerie screams. "So don't you blame me for this. Now, if everyone is waiting, as you said, let's go." Valerie grabs her suitcase, opens the door, and walks into the hallway. "Lock the door behind you," she yells at Ender.

"Valerie, I said you didn't need to pack anything," he yells back at her, slamming the door.

She stops and turns to face him. "Ender, I have nothing to wear there when we land. My choices are to wear the same things every day or run around your house naked until I can go shopping. Neither of those options appeals to me, and I certainly don't have a body like Melissa's." Valerie turns around and marches to the elevator. All Ender can do is follow, hanging his head.

Once in the elevator, Ender decides it would be best not to say anything else, so he stares at the floor. The tension in the elevator is so thick he almost can't breathe.

Exiting the building, Ender sees Joseph standing on the opposite side of the limo with a smile, which frustrates Ender even more. Ender watches Valerie to see what she will do, knowing he needs to stay out of her way.

The limo driver is sitting in the limo with his window rolled up. Valerie marches up to the limo and knocks on the driver's window, which he rolls down.

"Open up the back so I can put my suitcase in," Valerie demands.

"There wasn't supposed to be any luggage," the driver replies sharply.

"This isn't luggage. My suitcase is filled with lingerie, handcuffs, whips, canes, and a few sex toys. Now, will you open the back?"

Ender stands on the sidewalk, watching the events like an out-of-body experience. It takes a few seconds for Valerie's words to the driver to sink into Ender's brain. He watches as the driver searches frantically for the button to open the trunk. Joseph is laughing so hard tears run down his face. Valerie walks to the back of the limo, waiting for the trunk to be opened with her tote in one hand and the suitcase in the other.

Finally, Joseph stops laughing long enough to walk to the back of the limo and open the trunk. While he places the suitcase inside the car, Valerie walks around, opens the door, and climbs inside. Joseph gets in behind Valerie while Ender is still standing on the sidewalk with his headache and hangover, wondering what is going on.

Then the rear window rolls down, and Valerie yells, "Ender, get your ass in the car so we can go to the airport."

Ender shakes his head and gets inside the car just in time to see Valerie put her earbuds in and open her tablet. He looks at Murat, who has slept through the whole circus. Joseph is still laughing but trying hard to hold it inside. By now, the limo driver is a nervous wreck and pulls out in front of a car, almost wrecking the limo. Ender looks back at Valerie out of the corner of his eye. She is reading her tablet but is wearing a smirk. He lays his head back and wonders if this is his karma for spending two days and nights in Melissa's bed.

Not wanting to feel her wrath of Valerie again, Ender ensures he is the last to board his private jet. The flight attendant greets him warmly and informs him that Murat went into the smallest of the two bedrooms. Ender asks for a Bloody Mary, coffee, water, and ibuprofen. Next, he looks at where the others are seated. Fortunately, the plane is much larger than a standard private jet. Joseph is sitting close to the front, and Valerie is a few seats behind him. Ender heads for the back of the plane and sits facing the aircraft's rear.

He thinks about Valerie's comment to the limo driver concerning the suitcase's contents. Ender laughs loudly until his stomach hurts.

"You finally sobered up enough to appreciate what Valerie told the limo driver, didn't you?" Joseph turns around and yells over the plane's engines. All Ender can do is give Joseph a thumbs up. Joseph looks at Valerie, who winks and grins at him.

Ender spends his time looking through his phone, which was turned off while he was with Melissa. He finds all Valerie's messages and texts asking about flight information. He reads each one several times.

Two hours into the flight, everyone is served dinner. Finished, Joseph puts on headphones and begins watching a movie. When Ender sees the flight attendant collect Valerie's tray, he takes a deep breath and hesitantly approaches her. The seat Valerie selected faces forward, so Ender sits facing Valerie rather than beside her. She looks up at him and rolls her eyes when he sits down.

"What do you want, Ender?"

He reaches over and takes both of her hands in his. "I came to apologize. I'm very sorry I blamed you for something I messed up on."

"Okay. Apology accepted," Valerie says, looking down at her lap.

Ender moves forward in the seat until his knees touch hers. He lifts his hand to caress Valerie's cheek and then lifts her chin to force her to look at him. "I'm very sorry I yelled at you."

"You hurt me, Ender," Valerie says, tears filling her eyes.

"I don't understand," he whispers, moving his face closer to hers. "Let's go into the bedroom where we can talk privately."

"I don't think that's a very good idea."

"Trust me." Ender rises and pulls Valerie to her feet. He leads the way to the bedroom. "Here, you sit on the bed, and I'll sit in the chair. We'll leave the door open."

Valerie sits on the edge of the bed. Ender pulls the chair closer so he can reach her. Tears are rolling down her cheeks now. Ender reaches up and wipes them away tenderly.

"Valerie, please explain how I hurt you."

"You made me feel like I wasn't doing my job," Valerie replies.

"I read your texts and emails after we got on the plane. I can see why you feel that way. I'm sorry I hurt you, but I have to be honest. It won't be the last time," Ender says. "I've never been a person who considered other people's feelings. I wasn't brought up that way. I can try to do better, especially with you. I want to do better with you because you are special to me."

"Ender, I don't want to disappoint you. You took an enormous risk hiring me for this job."

"You haven't disappointed me. You impressed me because you caught on quickly. Now, what can I do to make this up to you? Would you like a diamond necklace, earrings, or something similar?"

"I want nothing except to be treated like a human being. That's all."

"But, Valerie, I can buy you anything and everything you could possibly want," Ender says.

"I'm not that kind of person, Ender. Material things are not important to me. People are."

"I will have to think about that. Now, we have about ten more hours of flight. Why don't you lie down here and sleep?"

"You need sleep more than I do," Valerie tells him.

"I have an idea." Ender walks to the front of the plane and gathers all the pillows he can find. He places them in a row in the middle of the bed when he returns. "Now," he says. "You sleep on one side, and I'll sleep on the other. We'll leave the door open." Valerie nods, removes her shoes and lies down.

Ender moves to the bathroom, and when he returns, Valerie is asleep. He covers her with a blanket and remains on the side of the bed next to her. Ender watches her sleep just like he did two years ago after laying her in his bed. She is more beautiful now than she was then, he thinks. After several minutes, he leans over and kisses Valerie's perfect lips softly. She opens her eyes slowly. Ender's nose is almost touching hers because he is so close. Valerie touches her lips.

"Ender, did you just kiss me?"

"Yes, just like I did the first time you were in my bed two years ago. I didn't mean to offend you. But your lips are just so perfect I couldn't resist," he answers. "One day, you will ask me to kiss you."

"You're my boss, and I'm not like Melissa."

"I know, Valerie," he whispers. "Believe me. I know you're not." Then Ender gets on his side of the bed and lies on his side, facing away from her. I want this woman to be mine, he decides, but what am I willing to give up to have her? The cost may be too great. Ender closes his eyes and dreams of Valerie in his bed, waiting for him.

Chapter 17

Valerie

The bounce of the plane on the runway wakes Valerie. She looks at her watch and decides they must be making a refueling stop. Valerie turns in the other direction and sees Ender asleep on his part of the bed and the wall of pillows. She touches her lips, remembering his gentle kiss. "Oh, Ender," she whispers. "If only I made you feel the way you make me feel when I'm with you." Valerie lies back and fantasizes about Ender holding her in his muscular arms and more. Soon she falls asleep again.

An hour later, Valerie wakes up feeling hot and weighted down. She looks down and finds Ender's arm lying over her stomach with his head on her shoulder. All the pillows that were stacked between them are gone.

"Ender. Ender, wake up."

"What?" he mutters.

"Please, Ender, wake up."

"Okay, Valerie." He opens his eyes. "What is it?"

"Did you move the pillows because they are gone?" Valerie asks.

"Not that I know of. Are you sure you didn't move them?"

"If I did, I don't remember. So what are we going to do?"

"I'm going back to sleep," Ender yawns and closes his eyes. "I suggest you do the same."

Ender does not turn over, so Valerie waits until his breathing slows. She carefully moves his head and arm. Finally, Valerie eases out of bed. She returns to the seat she had been sitting in and contemplates the time in the bedroom. Ender apologized for hurting her and said it would probably happen again. I'm sure of that. He thinks of no one but himself. He has no empathy toward people.

Next, Valerie thinks about Ender's kiss and touches her lips again. The kiss was so gentle. He said he did it two years ago. I don't remember that, so it must have been when I was knocked out with the pain injection. He also said I would ask him to kiss me one day. I doubt that. I'm not like Melissa or those other women, and I won't ever be. If only he weren't so handsome. I feel drawn to him somehow, but he's my boss. Relationships between a boss and an employee never turn out well.

Finally, she thinks about the pillows being gone when she woke up. Ender must have moved them because I know I didn't. It felt so lovely to have him sleeping next to me, though. Okay, that's enough thinking about Ender. I'm going to the bathroom and clean up a little. I see the sun coming up in the distance.

Valerie passes by the bed where Ender is still sleeping. She reaches down and moves a lock of hair from his face. At least in sleep, he doesn't have the cold eyes that harden his facial features. She moves on to the bathroom, where she takes a quick shower. Then she realizes she left her suitcase in the overhead compartment above her seat. Valerie wraps a towel around herself tightly and takes a deep breath. Quietly, Valerie eases open the door and peeks out. She sees and hears no one stirring, so she steps out. Looking around the corner, Valerie can tell Ender is still asleep. She creeps past the bed and looks down the aisle of the plane. She can see the top of Joseph's head.

Slowly, Valerie makes her way to retrieve the suitcase. Once she has it in hand, she anxiously rolls it toward the bathroom. Valerie keeps her eyes on the floor to ensure the suitcase doesn't bump into anything. Everything is going according to plan until she enters the bedroom doorway. Ender is sitting up in bed, watching every move she makes.

"Please tell me you're wearing that the rest of the flight," he says, with a broad grin and raised eyebrow.

Valerie turns a bright shade of red as she looks down at the towel covering her. "Uh, I'm sorry if I woke you," she stammers, frozen in place.

Ender climbs off the bed and stands, almost touching her. "I thought you said you weren't Melissa," he whispers. His hot breath touches her chest, giving her an idea of where his eyes are.

Anger overtakes embarrassment for Valerie. She looks up at Ender with the amber flecks flashing in her eyes. She lets go of the suitcase handle and raises her hand to slap him. But Ender catches her wrist in midair. He pulls her the short distance between them so Valerie's body is beside his. Valerie tries to push him away with her free hand, but Ender holds her tightly against him with his free arm. The grip on her wrist tightens as he twists her arm behind her.

Feeling defeated, Valerie relaxes her body against Ender and looks down. She feels her body wanting to melt against his. Valerie grows warm all over as desire takes over her body. She feels Ender's body react to her as well as he places his free hand on her behind and presses her against him.

"Ender, please let me go," Valerie whispers. Instead of answering, he places soft kisses along her neck and shoulders, causing her to shiver. Ender releases her wrist and runs his finger along the top of the towel, but he doesn't touch Valerie. Next, he places his hand under her chin, forcing Valerie to look into his eyes.

"Do you really want me to let you go?" he whispers, watching her eyes. Valerie doesn't answer because her brain is struggling with her body. "I asked you a question, Valerie." Finally, her brain wins, and Valerie nods her head. "Good girl," Ender says, releasing her. "Now, go get dressed."

Valerie hurries to the bathroom, dresses, and quickly returns to her seat. Ender is nowhere to be seen, thankfully. She lies back in her seat and takes deep breaths. Thank goodness my brain prevailed because I would have had

to quit my job and return to Miami tomorrow if I had let my body answer,
Valerie decides.

Chapter 18

Ender

Once Valerie enters the bathroom, Ender goes to the back of the plane, where a smaller bathroom is located. He passes by Murat, still asleep on the bed. Ender quietly closes the door and sits on the toilet, trying to slow his breathing and heart rate. My gosh, Valerie was so delicious standing there in that towel. She keeps telling me she's not Melissa. I just had to test her to see for myself. Valerie passed the test with flying colors, even though her body told a different story.

Ender turns the shower on, undresses, and then stands under the warm spray. He remembers the feel of Valerie's skin as he kissed her neck and shoulders and the fragrance of jasmine. Ender lets his mind wander over everything Valerie as he takes advantage of the shower, easing his physical need.

Weak from his release in the shower, Ender wraps a towel around himself and returns to the large bedroom and his walk-in closet. He dresses in jeans, a t-shirt, and sneakers. He then returns to the smaller bedroom and wakes an unhappy Murat.

"Why are you waking me? Are we home?" Murat mutters.

"We are about two hours away. You've slept the entire trip. It's time for you to get out of bed and clean up."

"I'll clean up at home, but I am hungry."

"As you wish. They will serve breakfast soon," Ender says.

"Ender, tell me about that beautiful woman you said is your personal assistant."

"There's nothing to tell. Valerie is efficient and a fast learner. Andrew is really impressed with her."

"What about you, Ender? Are you impressed with her?"

"Get your mind out of the gutter, Murat. My relationship with her is professional only," Ender replies.

"Well, you won't mind if I invite her to a night out in Istanbul. A night of dinner, partying, and lots of sex is good for the soul. But, of course, you know that as well as I do."

"Murat, I do mind. Go home to your wife and kids. My assistant isn't that kind of woman."

Murat laughs. "The only reason you would say that is if she's gay or turned you down already. Which is it?"

Ender gives Murat one of his icy stares as he stands and walks out of the room. "Get up and come to the front of the plane if you want to eat."

Ender sits at the back of the plane during breakfast. He sends and reads messages and emails until the plane lands. He looks out the window, pleased that Andrew received his messages and did what he asked. Finally, Ender stands and walks to Valerie's seat. "Valerie, we can deplane now," he says, motioning her to exit first. He senses her confusion at the bottom of the steps as three vehicles pull up to the plane. Murat hurries past everyone and waves as he climbs into a small sporty car.

"Joseph, take Ms. Richards' suitcase with you and put it into the large suite on the second floor. Ms. Richards is coming with me." Ender puts his hand on the small of Valerie's back, guiding her to a sporty convertible. He notices her shiver as he opens the door for her and says, "let's have some fun."

Since the private airport is outside of Istanbul, it takes thirty minutes to drive downtown. Ender pulls up to the curb, hands the valet his keys, and ushers Valerie into a large designer clothing store. The pair are approached by a store representative quickly. Ender points to several chairs and instructs Valerie to sit down. After she does, he and the representative walk through various women's clothing displays.

Finally, after an hour, Ender walks over to Valerie. "I have selected several things for you. I'll let you choose your personal items. I have an errand to run. I'll be back in a couple of hours." He reaches into his shirt pocket. "Here," he says, handing Valerie two credit cards. "Use the one in your name to pay for everything. The other is for business purchases." Ender turns and walks away.

Chapter 19

Valerie

Valerie watches her handsome boss walk away and notices the sales representative watching him as well. Then, she looks down at the credit cards Ender handed her. The cards are the most exclusive credit cards anyone can carry. Valerie has seen advertisements for these cards but never dreamed she would hold one. Especially one with her name on it.

"Shall we get started?" the sales representative asks.

Three hours later, Valerie emerges from a fitting room to find Ender sitting nearby, reading a newspaper. "Are you finished?" he asks, looking up from the paper.

"Yes, but I need a few minutes to decide what to take with me now," Valerie replies.

"Be sure to select a nice dress for tonight," he says.

"Oh, okay." Valerie turns to the sales representative. "When will the clothing be delivered?" The woman answers early tomorrow morning, so Valerie selects a bikini, a coverup, some lingerie, and a yellow off-the-shoulder dress that hits her mid-thigh. Last, she selects three pairs of shoes. Finally, she walks up to Ender holding several bags, and says, "I'm finished."

"Great. I'll carry your bags." Ender reaches for the bags, leads Valerie to the car, and helps her inside. "Are you hungry?"

"Not really, but I'll eat something if you are," Valerie answers.

"I'm not ready to eat, so we'll go home. There'll be something we can snack on if we get hungry later." Valerie nods. "Valerie, I have something serious I need to discuss with you. I guess now is as good a time as any. Word will travel fast that you are working with me. I have a few acquaintances here and many enemies who would love to see me destroyed or hurt. It would be best if you went nowhere alone, including Miami. So I am assigning Joseph to be your personal bodyguard."

"Ender, is that really necessary? I'm just an assistant of yours."

He reaches over and takes Valerie's hand in his. "You are very important to me and my business. I'm not willing to take a chance on anything happening to you. If Joseph can't be with you, Burak will be. Those are the two men I trust the most with your safety."

"Okay, Ender. I guess I never thought about you being in danger, but since you are a busy, important man, it makes sense," Valerie says with a smile and squeezes his hand.

Ender laughs aloud. "Oh, one more thing, Valerie. Will you have dinner with me tonight at the house? Not a working dinner, but a friendly dinner?"

"I would like that, Ender. Is that why you had me pick a dress?"

"Yes. Now, let's go for a ride and enjoy what's left of this beautiful morning." Ender releases Valerie's hand, turns on the radio, and drives away from the city.

Wearing the sunglasses Ender gave her, Valerie sits back and enjoys the wind in her hair and the music in her ears. She hasn't felt this relaxed in a very long time. Occasionally, Valerie glances at Ender out of the corner of her eye and notices he looks calm and at ease. When she looks over at him, he turns to her and smiles.

After two hours of driving, Ender drives up a large hill to a house at the top. Joseph and Burak come out of the house to meet them.

"Welcome to your Istanbul home, Valerie," Ender says, proudly waving his arm across the property.

"Oh my. This is beautiful. Did you design the house?"

"Yes, but I had help decorating it," Ender replies. "Let me give you a tour of the inside, and we'll do the outside later." Then, curious about Valerie's earlier reaction, he places his palm on the small of her back and again feels her shiver.

Ender quickly guides her through the downstairs area, pointing out the living area, library/game room, kitchen, dining area, his office, and suite. Next, he takes Valerie upstairs to her suite. Ender hears her sharp intake of breath as he opens the door.

"Ender, this is the size of a normal house," Valerie says in awe. "This is too much for me."

"Nonsense. While you're here, you will probably make friends and need a place to entertain them. You'll want your privacy too. There may be instances where I have guests, and you'll also want your privacy."

Valerie turns to look at Ender. "So you have a Turkish version of Melissa, or do you fly her over here?"

"Valerie, my personal life is not your concern," Ender replies sharply.

"You're right. I'm sorry, Ender." Valerie looks down at the floor.

Ender says nothing but takes her hand and leads her to the windows overlooking the property. "I have an infinity pool if you want to swim this afternoon. Dinner will be at 7:00. I'll meet you at the bottom of the stairs." He drops her hand and leaves as Joseph walks in carrying her shopping bags.

"Valerie, if Mr. Dogan didn't show you, the closet is to your right. I put your suitcase in there."

"Thanks, Joseph. Ender said he was assigning you to be my personal bodyguard. Is that really necessary?"

"Yes, ma'am. It is, I'm sorry to say. Perhaps you should have been told about the potential dangers before taking this job, but it wasn't my place to advise you."

"It's okay, Joseph. I trust you and your judgment. But if I step out of line, please don't be afraid to remind me, okay?"

"Okay, Valerie. Is there anything I can get for you?"

"No, I think I'll change and go for a swim. Thank you for everything, Joseph."

Chapter 20

Ender

Leaving Valerie, Ender goes to his office and sits at his desk, somewhat pleased with himself. He picked out some very nice clothes for Valerie. She will look great in all of it. The drive was so relaxing after his uncomfortable discussion with her about security. Valerie could easily be a potential target. That's why he's giving her Joseph. Joseph has not only been my best friend since college, but he is also highly trained ex-military, Ender thinks. I wouldn't trust anyone else with Valerie's safety. I hope she isn't her usual hard-headed self and will heed my warning.

Ender leans back in his chair and looks out the window toward the infinity pool. Standing at the edge of the pool is Valerie wearing a see thru white coverup. Unaware he's holding his breath, Ender watches as Valerie turns her back toward him and removes the robe. When she lays it down on the chaise, her swimsuit rides up her butt slightly. As she stands, she pulls the suit down and turns around slowly.

Ender's eyes start at the top of Valerie's head. Her brown hair is pulled back in a ponytail showing off the narrow neck he kissed this morning. The red one-piece swimsuit has oval cutouts from below her breasts to below her navel. Valerie's legs are long, even though she's five foot two. Ender watches as she daintily sticks one foot into the water as if testing the temperature. As he observes Valerie, Ender marvels at how the suit accentuates her curves. Wow! Her body is as perfect as her lips, he decides.

As Valerie bends at the waist and dives into the pool, the top of the suit lowers, showing an extensive amount of cleavage. "No, Ms. Richards, you are nothing like Melissa," Ender says aloud. "Everything about you is 100% all natural." When Valerie breaks the water's surface, she glides through the pool smoothly several times. All Ender can do is watch, mesmerized. Finally, Valerie climbs out of the pool and grabs a towel. Ender licks his lips as she dries herself off. When Valerie lies back on the chaise, Ender watches for a few minutes and then swiftly walks to his bathroom to release the tension that has built up in him.

Ender stays in the bathroom for quite a while because once his tension is released, it builds again quickly with his thoughts of Valerie. He is as weak as a newborn kitten when he is finally spent and returns to his chair. Valerie is no longer by the pool. Thank goodness she's gone. I couldn't take anymore, Ender thinks. He crosses his arms on the top of his desk and lays his head down. His mind wanders back to Valerie's question about a Turkish Melissa, or does he fly Melissa here? Valerie has brought up Melissa several times. Could Valerie be jealous? If I wanted to have Valerie in my bed regularly, would I have to give up Melissa or the other women? Could I give them up? Could I be a one-woman man? I wasn't with my ex-wife.

"Ender. Ender, wake up. Aren't you having dinner with Ms. Richards at 7:00?"

Ender opens his eyes and finds Joseph standing next to him. "Yeah, 7:00."

"Well, it's 6:00 now, so you better hurry."

"Okay. I guess I fell asleep. Is everything ready?"

"It will be by 6:30," Joseph answers, turning and walking away.

Dressed in a white linen shirt and pants, Ender waits anxiously for Valerie at the bottom of the stairs. He's been there for twenty minutes, pacing back and forth. Then, finally, he hears a sound and looks up at the top of the stairs. A smiling Valerie stands in a short yellow off-the-shoulder dress with matching sandals. Her brown hair is pulled back into a bun. Ender's heart races at the sight of her.

"Is this okay?" Valerie asks. "I wasn't sure what your plans were."

"Valerie, you look stunning and perfect." Ender holds out his hand, inviting her to join him. Ender places a soft kiss on her cheek when she reaches him. Then he offers her his arm, and they walk together to the patio.

Torches surround the patio, giving off soft light. In the center of the patio is a table set for two with glowing candles. Soft music is playing in the background. The evening is warm with a slight breeze.

"Ender, this is beautiful," Valerie says, looking up at him.

"Thank you. Will you dance with me?" Ender asks. Valerie nods shyly.

Ender takes her hand in his and places his other hand on the small of her back, feeling her shiver. Valerie places her hand on his bicep, keeping a safe distance between them. Ender discovers she is an excellent dancer as he leads her around the patio.

After three dances, Ender suggests they eat. While they eat, he asks about Valerie's life. She tells him she grew up in Montana and left after graduation for the warmer climate of Arizona. Her parents are both gone, and she is an only child. When Ender asks how Valerie ended up in Miami, she explains she always wanted to live close to a beach and followed her college boyfriend to Miami. They broke up six months later.

Ender tells her he, too, is an only child. His parents were from Turkey, and he was born there. After graduating, he moved to Southern California to study engineering. He got bored and changed his major to finance. He met Joseph in college. After college graduation, Ender returned to Turkey to start his business. Joseph joined the US Army. Ender hired Joseph as head of security when Joseph got out of the military.

"Valerie, have you ever been married or in a serious, long-term relationship?" Ender asks.

"I've never been married. I was in a serious relationship for a year, but he became very abusive, and I had to leave. You said you have an ex-wife. Do you have kids, Ender?"

"No, kids. I wanted none and still don't. I don't like kids."

"Oh, okay. I want kids someday, but not soon," Valerie says.

"Valerie, I have something for you." Ender reaches into his pocket and hands Valerie a small jeweler's box.

"Ender, you didn't have to do this."

"Yes, I did. Open it, please." Valerie opens it to find a beautiful necklace in the shape of a star with a small amber stone in the center. "Turn it over," Ender says. She does and looks a little confused. "You always wear your bracelet that says you're allergic to shellfish. Although medically necessary, it's not very attractive. This necklace tells about your allergy in English and Turkish. I felt it was necessary since you will be here so much. The amber stone matches the amber flecks in your eyes when you get angry," Ender finishes with a smile.

"Ender, I never would have thought about that. Thank you so much."

"Would you like me to put it on for you?"

"Yes, please," Valerie replies, removing the necklace from the box and handing it to him.

Ender places the necklace around her neck and fastens it, careful not to touch Valerie as he does. He inhales her jasmine scent deeply and exhales, purposely blowing his warm breath on her bare neck.

"Thank you," Valerie whispers. Ender knows he's had the effect on her he desired.

"Come with me," Ender says, offering his hand. Valerie takes it. He leads her to the far end of the patio. "Valerie, here you have all of Istanbul at your feet." Ender points toward the city, shining in all its glory below them. "And above you, all the stars in the heavens." He points upward.

Valerie looks at all the city's lights and then into the clear night sky. She looks up for a long time. Ender is still holding Valerie's hand and feels her falter. He quickly puts his arm around her waist, pulling her closer.

"Valerie, are you okay?"

"Yes, I looked up too long and got a little dizzy."

"What were you thinking about?"

"I was wondering if there's a man somewhere out there for me. It's silly, I know," Valerie answers.

"What kind of man are you hoping for?" Ender whispers.

"A man that is kind and gentle. He makes me the center of his universe. I am the only woman in his world, and he is the only man in mine." Valerie turns toward him. "What kind of woman are you hoping for, Ender?"

"I do not know. I never thought about it," Ender replies. "It's late. Tomorrow is a workday for me. I want you to take the day off and do whatever you wish. We will get back on track tomorrow night." He releases Valerie, turns, and walks off, leaving her alone on the patio.

Joseph follows Ender into his office. "What the hell are you doing, Ender?" he demands.

"What do you mean?"

"You're making her fall in love with you. That's what I mean. She's too good for you, and you know it. You'll only hurt her badly, and she'll be gone forever."

"Joseph, she is not falling in love with me, and I certainly am not falling for her," Ender growls.

Joseph puts his hands on the desk and leans over. "Then what are you doing?"

"I don't know, Joseph. I really don't know," Ender says, combing his fingers through his hair. "Besides, I'm not the kind of man she's looking for."

"I heard what she said, and I agree you're not at all what she wants. However, I don't think you can ever be a one-woman man. You're too greedy, and your personal desires are almost as important as your business. So leave her alone, Ender. Goodnight." Joseph stomps off.

Ender looks at the clock and picks up the phone. There's only one thing that can get Valerie off his mind. The phone is answered on the first ring. "Aylin, are you free tonight because I need you to soothe my aching body?" The woman answers yes. Ender hangs up the phone, grabs his car keys, and heads out to his convertible. Once in the car, he looks up to see Valerie standing at her window, watching him. He shakes his head and leaves, heading toward Istanbul and Aylin. Aylin always takes good care of Ender's body and frees his mind.

Chapter 21

Valerie

Valerie stands at the window, fingering the star on the necklace Ender gave her. That was so thoughtful of him, she thinks. I would never have thought about needing my allergy information in Turkish. She looks down and sees Ender getting into his car. He seems to be in a hurry, she thinks. He looks up at her and drives off.

I guess he's off to see his Turkish version of Melissa. Why does that bother me so much? Because you're jealous, a tiny voice in her head answers. He's not the man for you. You will only get hurt because he can't be with only one woman. Besides, you will lose this fantastic job, and then where will you be?

Valerie changes into a bikini she brought with her and wraps a towel around her. She goes to the kitchen and finds an almost full bottle of wine in the fridge. Valerie searches for a glass among the many cabinets. Finally, she finds one and takes it and the bottle to the patio. Valerie pours a glass of wine, drops the towel, and climbs into the hot tub.

"Valerie. Valerie." Valerie squints her eyes slowly to find Ender shaking her.

"What time is it?"

"It is 4:00 am. Did you drink the entire bottle of wine?" Ender asks. Valerie giggles. "No wonder you're sleeping on the patio. Place your arms around my neck." Valerie does as Ender lifts her out of the chair.

"You smell good," Valerie says as Ender carries her into the house. "Funny, you smell like yourself instead of a woman. I guess you showered before you came home."

"Valerie, what am I going to do with you?" Ender asks.

"I have several ideas," Valerie answers as he carries her up the stairs. She nuzzles his neck. "Do you like my bikini?" Valerie giggles.

"Yes, Valerie. I like your bikini, what little there is of it. Maybe you should wear it in the daytime when I can see it better."

"Okay, I'll wear it tomorrow."

When they reach her bedroom, Ender sits Valerie in a chair so he can turn back the covers on the bed. "Valerie, you're drunk and wet. I'm going to turn around now. You take off your bikini and climb into bed, okay?"

"Okay, Ender," Valerie replies. Ender turns around to give her some privacy. She stands, crumples to the floor, and giggles.

Ender turns around. "Valerie, I didn't want to do this, but you've given me no choice." He helps her off the floor. Holding Valerie up with one arm, Ender unties the strings on the bikini, letting it fall to the floor. He picks her up and lays her down on the bed.

As he starts to cover her, Valerie giggles. "Do you like what you see, Ender?" He does not comment and pulls the covers up to her neck as she watches him. "Kiss me, Ender," Valerie says. "I need you to kiss me."

"Not like this, Valerie. I want you sober when I do."

"You don't want me," Valerie cries.

Ender leans down and kisses her on the forehead. "I wish you too much, baby." Then he turns off the light and leaves.

Valerie closes her eyes as Ender's words repeatedly roll through her mind until she falls asleep.

Chapter 22

Ender

All I wanted to do was to come home and go to bed. Aylin wore me out. But, no, it couldn't be that simple. I come home to find a drunk Valerie passed out by the pool. Thank goodness she didn't fall in and drown. Then I had to put her to bed and deal with drunken talk.

"Yes, Valerie, I didn't just like what I saw; I loved it when I had to take off your bikini. Yes, I wanted you to ask me to kiss you, but not when you're drunk. But I didn't lie to you when I said I wanted you too much. The whole time I was with Aylin, you were on my mind. Now, Valerie, get out of my head so I can sleep a couple of hours," Ender finishes his conversation with imaginary Valerie and climbs into bed.

Ender drags himself up and sits on the edge of the bed when the alarm goes off. The two hours he slept were filled with visions of Valerie in his bed. Finally, he looks down at his lap and says, "it's all your fault. Between Valerie and the other women, I'm going to wear you out."

After a shower and relieving himself, Ender dresses and leaves quickly, wanting to avoid Valerie. He has a busy day today and needs a clear head. So Burak drives him to the office while Ender naps on the way.

Chapter 23

Valerie

Valerie wakes with a headache and parched mouth when there's a knock on her door. She's hoping it's Ender, but it turns out to be Joseph bearing gifts of coffee, water, ibuprofen, dry toast, and something red in a glass.

"Good morning, Valerie. Drink the red stuff first. Then take the ibuprofen with water. Next, drink the coffee while you eat the toast."

"Joseph, how did you know?" Valerie asks, embarrassed.

"There are security cameras everywhere, luckily for you. Burak and I would have seen and saved you if you had fallen in the pool. As it is, you fell asleep, and Ender saved you."

"Oh no. I hope I didn't do or say anything stupid to him."

"You did nothing in the pool area. There are no cameras in here, so you're safe there. Ender knows the cameras record voices, so when he talked to you, he talked low enough that we didn't hear a thing," Joseph says.

"How am I going to face him after last night?"

"You have all day to figure that out. He left early this morning. Now, do what I told you. I'll be back in an hour to discuss what you might like to do today."

Valerie does as Joseph says and lies back down. If Ender left early this morning, that's a bad sign. It means he wanted to avoid her. I wish I could remember what I said. I'm sure I embarrassed myself. But did he really say I want you too much, baby, or did I dream that? I bet I dreamed it because that's nothing Ender Dogan would say to me or any woman. He's not that kind of man.

When Joseph returns, he suggests going to the art gallery where he knocked her down two years ago. He tells her the exhibits have changed and she would enjoy it.

As Valerie and Joseph walk through the art exhibits, Valerie says, "you don't really have a social life, do you?"

"There's not much time for things like that in my world."

"I noticed you and Andrew spend a lot of time together."

"He's a good friend," Joseph answers.

"Does Ender know?" Valerie asks, looking up at the tough man standing beside her. Joseph looks down at her and shakes his head. She reaches for his hand and squeezes it tightly. "Hold my hand, Joseph. I'll never let go, no matter what." Tears fill his eyes. They continue to walk through the gallery, holding hands and laughing.

At 6:58, Valerie heads downstairs for dinner dressed in one of the new outfits Ender picked out. It is a light green crop top with white slacks. Ender is nowhere to be seen. Valerie sits her tote down in the chair next to her and takes out everything she needs for their meeting. She waits until 7:10 and begins filling her plate. Ender appears when Valerie is almost finished eating.

"I apologize for being late."

"No apology needed, Ender. I have nothing to discuss except what you plan to wear to your ex-wife's wedding tomorrow."

"I forgot about that joyous occasion," Ender replies, filling his plate with food. "I'll just wear my navy suit."

"With a white shirt, of course." Valerie looks at her plate and smirks.

"Why don't you go tomorrow and buy me a shirt and tie that you think might be better," Ender says sarcastically, looking at Valerie with his cold, hard eyes.

"I think I will do just that, Mr. Dogan. If you have nothing further to discuss, then I declare this meeting over," Valerie states. She stands and carries her plate to the kitchen. When she returns, she picks up everything and stomps out of the room.

Once in her room, Valerie changes into a one-piece swimsuit and heads to the pool. She dives right into the pool and swims several laps before pausing at the side of the pool overlooking the city. Valerie hears a splash behind her and knows it's Ender. She hesitates for a few seconds and then reaches for the ladder to climb out. As she reaches up, an arm grabs hers and jerks her body around. Ender pins Valerie against the side of the pool.

"You ended our meeting. It appears you have forgotten who you work for," Ender says.

"So I suppose you're going to remind me by giving me one of your cold, hard stares." Valerie stares directly into his eyes, waiting.

"No, I'm going to remind you like this," Ender's hand grips the back of Valerie's head as his lips meet hers. It isn't a tender kiss but a demanding one. It takes a second for Valerie to realize what's happening. Then her body begins to respond. First, her fingers caress Ender's face and then move upward, running through his hair. Next, Valerie's other hand goes to his shoulder. Finally, she pushes her body into his. Ender pulls back in surprise and looks at Valerie.

"Ender, I want you to kiss me, but not like this," Valerie says as the amber flecks spark. She uses all her strength to push him away and climbs out of the pool. Valerie grabs a towel and walks away, knowing Ender is watching her.

Chapter 24

Ender

Damn that woman, Ender says to himself as he climbs out of the pool. I intended to teach her a lesson, but she took control of the situation and me. He sits down on a chaise and holds his head in his hands. He lies back on the chaise, watching the stars, hoping for an answer. After a while, he decides that no response is forthcoming and to go to bed. He looks up and sees Valerie watching him from her window. She smiles, blows him a kiss, and pulls the drapes.

Ender thinks about calling Aylin again, but he really needs to sleep. He is running on nothing but adrenaline right now, and it's wearing him down fast. So he strips off his swim trunks and climbs into bed, falling asleep immediately, even though it is only 8:30.

The following day, Ender leaves the office at noon. The wedding festivities begin at 3:00, so he needs time to clean up and dress. When he walks into his bedroom, he finds his navy suit lying on the bed. Next to it is a pale blue shirt with a white tie. Ender smiles, knowing Valerie bought the shirt and tie this morning. He walks into his closet, surprised to find several new shirts and ties in various colors and patterns. Well, it appears Ms. Richards was busy this morning; he thinks.

Ender expects to see Valerie when he enters the kitchen for lunch, but she's nowhere around. So after he dresses, he climbs the stairs, finding her bedroom door open with Valerie staring at an empty wall.

"Good afternoon, Valerie."

"Wow, Ender. Don't you look handsome in your new shirt and tie?" Valerie says with a smirk. "I need to straighten your tie, though." Valerie grabs a nearby stepstool she's been using to hang pictures and places it in front of Ender. She steps onto it and straightens his tie. "Turn around, Ender."

He turns and looks into a full-length mirror. Valerie places both hands on his biceps and her chin on his right shoulder.

"The groom will so be envious of how handsome you are," Valerie says, her eyes meeting Ender's in the mirror.

"I doubt that, but I look pretty good," Ender says, adjusting his cuffs while still gazing into Valerie's eyes. "Thank you, Valerie. I always knew you'd bring a little color into my life. I just never thought it would be clothing."

Valerie drops her hands and steps back off the stool. She bends down to pick it up while Ender turns around. Both reach for the stool simultaneously, and their noses are almost touching.

"Ask me," Ender whispers.

"Ask you what?"

"Ask me to kiss you. I know you want me to."

"I shouldn't have to ask. If you want to kiss me, then do. Otherwise, stop teasing me," Valerie replies, standing and walking away.

Ender stands and clears his throat. "Turkish weddings seem to go on forever," he says, changing the subject. "I don't know when I'll be home, so we won't meet tonight."

"That's fine with me. I have things to do," Valerie replies with her back to him.

"Valerie, I have a favor to ask of you. I have that ball tomorrow night, and I had planned to take a date. But, unfortunately, I've been so busy I forgot to ask anyone. Would you go with me?"

"You're kidding, right?" Ender shakes his head. "You want me to go to a ball with you, and you're telling me about it the day before?" The amber flecks shoot out of Valerie's eyes.

"I'm not kidding, and you know these things might occur as part of your job. Wear the cream-colored gown with gold threads. The gold matches the sparks in your eyes right now. We will leave at 6:30 tomorrow night." Ender turns and walks out.

"Sometimes I hate you," Valerie yells at the top of her lungs.

"But, most of the time, you love me like crazy," Ender yells back.

The wedding festivities went on forever. First, there was a social hour followed by the ceremony. Next came dinner and dancing. Finally, at 11:00 pm, Ender found a reason to leave. Aylin was there and was just as eager to go as he was. It didn't take long for the clothes to disappear after arriving at Aylin's apartment. However, nothing Aylin did could erase the thoughts of Valerie from Ender's mind. Her chin on his shoulder, her jasmine fragrance, the way she shivers when Ender touches her, and most of all, Valerie's perfect lips that beg to be kissed. Ender finally gave up and left for home at 2:00 am.

Chapter 25

Ender

"Are you almost finished?" Ender yells from the bottom of the stairs. "We need to leave in ten minutes." Frustrated at having to wait, Ender turns around when Joseph enters to tell him the car is waiting downstairs. When Ender notices Joseph looking up at the stairs and smiling, he spins around, unsure of what to expect.

Valerie stands at the top of the stairs in the strapless, form-fitting evening gown Ender chose. Her hair is up, revealing the silky skin of her neck and shoulders. One hand holds an evening bag with a wrap draped over the arm. The other hand sits lightly on the railing of the stairs.

"You don't have to yell, Mr. Dogan. I'm right here," Valerie says with a smile on her red, cupid, bow-shaped lips. She slowly makes her way down the steps to where Ender is waiting. "Does this meet your approval?" Valerie asks, looking up at Ender.

He decides she must wear five-inch heels because he doesn't have to look down as far. "You look stunning, Ms. Richards. I'm tempted to stay home and just stare at you all night long."

Valerie huffs. "I don't think so. Well, let's go since you are in such a hurry."

Ender nods, takes her arm and leads her to the elevator.

Valerie appeared to enjoy herself at the ball; Ender ponders on the ride home. Most of the people he introduced her to spoke English, so Valerie could converse with them. For those that didn't speak English, Ender translated for her. Valerie was the perfect date for Ender. She was always pleasant and slightly affectionate when needed. Ender was proud of the appreciative looks Valerie received from the other men at the ball. She was also a marvelous dancer, and Ender's body stayed on high alert as he held her in his arms.

After returning to the apartment, Valerie removes her shoes and climbs the stairs to her bedroom while Ender watches from the kitchen. He pours a drink and takes his first sip.

"Ender, would you come up and help me for a minute?" A smile creeps across his lips, and he rushes up the steps. As he steps into Valerie's bedroom, she asks, "would you mind unzipping me? I can't reach it."

"Sure, I'll be happy to help." Ender walks behind her and reaches for the zipper, but not before running his finger along her spine to reach it. He notices Valerie is standing in front of the full-length mirror, watching him. Ender drags the zipper down, positioning his fingers between Valerie's skin and the material of the dress as he does. He feels her shiver.

When he's finished, he looks into the mirror and into her eyes. Valerie's brown eyes are dark, and there is a sensual look about her, Ender notices, even though she is holding the top of her gown up with one arm. He kisses the back of her neck and hears Valerie moan. Then, he pulls the pins from her hair, freeing the brown locks to fall on her shoulders. Next, Ender puts his hands on her hips and turns Valerie around to face him. Her eyes are closed, and she licks her lips. Ender brushes the hair off one shoulder and starts kissing the spot under Valerie's ear.

"Ask me, baby," he whispers as his tongue softly teases the outline of her ear. "Please, ask me. I want to kiss you so badly."

"Ender, please," is all Valerie can say before a voice calls from downstairs.

"Mr. Dogan, you have a visitor," Burak says.

Ender continues to hold on to Valerie and says, "I'm not expecting anyone."

"I know, but you better see who it is," Burak replies.

"Stay just as you are. I'll be right back," Ender whispers in Valerie's ear.

Ender hurries down the stairs and finds Aylin standing at the elevator. He nods to Burak, who leaves the two alone. In Turkish, Ender asks Aylin what she's doing there. First, she flies into his arms and kisses him deeply. Then, she answers he didn't get his money's worth last night, and she's there to make things right. Aylin backs up, opens her coat, and reveals her naked body. Ender tells her to cover herself and follow him. He turns to lead Aylin to the kitchen and looks up at the stairs. Valerie is standing there, still holding the bodice of her dress up with one arm, waiting for him to return. Only this time, there are tears in her eyes.

Hurrying into the kitchen with Aylin, Ender explains that tonight is not a good time for Aylin to be there and she should leave. But Aylin wants to argue, which frustrates Ender. The time that he could be with Valerie is being wasted. Finally, he grabs Aylin by the arm and pushes her to the elevator. He waits until she is inside, then runs upstairs to Valerie, but she isn't there.

Ender searches the entire house but still doesn't find her. So finally, with no other choice, he searches for Joseph or Burak. Together, all three watch the video feed from the security cameras and see Valerie walk from the patio into the garden. At that point, they lose sight of her. Joseph and Burak offer to find her, but Ender tells them no. Instead, he will go after her.

Grabbing a flashlight, Ender heads to the garden. Unfortunately, the garden is extensive and is not lit, so it takes an hour to find Valerie sitting on a bench behind the jasmine bushes Ender had planted last year.

"Go away, Ender," Valerie says as he sits beside her on the bench.

"Valerie, I'm sorry. I did not know she would visit tonight."

"Visit?" Valerie says sharply. "Is that what you call it when your Turkish Melissa shows up? You're nothing more than a whore monger, aren't you? No matter who she is, you will never be satisfied with one woman."

Ender can tell by Valerie's voice she's been crying. He places his arm on the back of the bench and tries to pull her close.

"Don't you dare touch me with a whore's lipstick on your lips and her perfume on your clothes," Valerie spews and then takes a deep breath. "Ender, I will never be enough woman for you. I don't know why I thought I could be. So just fire me and send me back to Miami, where I belong."

"Valerie, I don't want to lose you as an employee, so firing you is out of the question."

"You just don't get it. The only part of what I said that registers with you is the business part. Please, just go. I want to be alone."

Ender hesitates before getting up. "I'll leave the flashlight with you," he tells her as he stands. "I don't have what you want from me."

"And I don't know what you want from me," Valerie says, turning on the bench, so her back is to Ender.

Ender slowly returns to the house and goes to bed, but he can't sleep. He's still angry with Aylin for just showing up at his home and interrupting his time with Valerie. He's confused by Valerie's business comment, so he replays the conversation in his head. Many could consider him a whore monger, as Valerie called him. But he only used them for release and occasional dates. Can he help it if he likes sex? What was it Valerie said? She would never be enough woman for him, and she didn't know why she thought she could be. Did that mean she wanted to be enough? Oh, no wonder she made the comment about business. He said he didn't want to fire her, but he said nothing about her being enough of a woman for him. I need to listen better to what Valerie says. Now, how am I going to fix this mess?

Chapter 26

Valerie

After Ender leaves, Valerie sits alone in the garden for several minutes before she hears a twig snap behind her.

"Ender, I told you to leave me alone."

"It's me," Joseph says. "I thought you might get cold, so I brought you a blanket."

"Thanks, Joseph."

"Would you like me to sit with you awhile?"

"No, but thanks. I won't be much longer," Valerie answers.

"Okay, but I'll wait for you, so I know you make it back to the house. Good night, Valerie."

"Good night, Joseph."

Valerie lies down on the bench and wraps the blanket around her. Finally, weariness overtakes her, and she falls asleep.

The words "put your arms around my neck," wakes Valerie. She does, and muscular arms lift her. Valerie lays her head against the man's neck and inhales her favorite cologne. What a pleasant dream, she thinks as she's carried into the house and upstairs to her bedroom. The man lays her on the bed, covers her, and climbs beside her. He leans over and softly kisses her lips before pulling her into his arms and holding her tightly.

The ping of her phone wakes Valerie. She snuggles under the covers, re-membering her dream of being carried by muscular arms to her bed, a soft kiss on the lips, and a man holding her tightly as she fell asleep. Valerie turns her head to reach for her phone. The scent of her favorite men's cologne hits her nose. She smells of her pillow and the pillow next to her. Then she notices the smell on her nightgown. It wasn't a dream after all. It was Ender caring for her when he should have been sleeping.

Filled with hope and a little residual anger, Valerie checks the message on her phone. "Today is the day to tour the office. We leave at 9:00." Oh wow! I get to go to the Istanbul office today. How exciting! Oh, no. It's 7:30. I better hurry. Valerie jumps in the shower. She's getting ready to dry her hair when another text message comes in. "HELP! NOW!"

Valerie looks in the mirror. She has a towel around her body and one around her hair, but Ender needs help. I hope he didn't fall or something. She rushes downstairs and knocks on his bedroom door. When there's no answer, she fears the worst, opens the door, and walks in.

"Ender! Ender, are you okay?"

"Yes, I'm fine," he answers with a huge grin. He stands in the bathroom's doorway. He is wearing nothing but a towel, shaving cream covers half his face, and his hair is a mess.

Valerie gawks at him for several seconds and then shakes her head, hoping the blood will quickly run from below her waist back to her brain. "Thank goodness. I got your text and was afraid you fell or something. What did you need?"

"Well, you did such a great job picking out my clothes for the wedding. I thought you might want to pick them out today."

"Oh, okay," Valerie stammers. "Do you have any big meetings today?" she asks, walking to Ender's closet.

"Yes, I have an important meeting with Ms. Richards this morning. I plan to tour the office and then show her the Miami hotel project model."

Valerie rolls her eyes, walks into the closet, and surveys the suits. She selects a dark gray one and turns to lay it on the bed. But when she turns around,

Ender, still only dressed in a towel, is leaning against the doorframe of the closet. Valerie walks past him without looking at him. After laying the suit on the bed, she returns to the closet to select a shirt. She can feel Ender watching her every movement.

Selecting a light gray shirt with darker gray stripes takes a few minutes. Valerie lays the shirt on the bed and returns to the closet for a tie. Since Ender is making her nervous, Valerie decides to skip the tie. She walks to the closet door, but just when she gets there, Ender raises his arm, blocking her way.

"No tie today?" he says in a low voice.

"I don't think so since you don't have any important meetings."

"That will definitely be a change for me and interesting for everyone in the office. You know what else would be interesting, Valerie?"

"What's that?"

"I think it would be interesting to see what's under that towel you're wearing?"

Valerie snorts. "I doubt that."

"Why, Valerie?" Ender whispers in her ear.

"First, you've seen most of it when I wore a bikini. I think you've seen all of it when you put me to bed the night I got drunk. Second, you would find it boring because it isn't surgically enhanced after what I saw last night."

"Why don't you let me decide?" Ender's warm breath tickles her ear.

Valerie grins at him. "I think what's under your towel might be interesting." Then she ducks under his arm and walks away.

Ender watches Valerie walk away. Well, she's right. I have seen all of her under the circumstances she described. He rubs his freshly shaved jaw. It definitely wasn't boring, although I didn't stand and stare at her. I wanted to touch and kiss her, all of her. I still do. He sighs. At least she hasn't lost her sense of humor teasing him with her last comment. I hope one day she will find me interesting too.

Valerie is wearing black slacks and a red sleeveless blouse when she comes down the stairs. Over her arm is a white jacket.

"Very professional, Ms. Richards," Ender says. "How do I look?"

Valerie looks at him from top to bottom. "You need to unbutton the collar and the next button. Let a little of your muscular chest show along with a little of the blond hair you have." As soon as the last words flow from her lips, Valerie turns a bright shade of pink.

"Ms. Richards, are you blushing?" Valerie looks at the floor. Ender unbuttons the top two buttons and then says, "I'm flattered you've noticed my chest, muscles and all. Maybe one day you can touch it." He points to the elevator, and they both enter.

"You need to stop teasing me," Valerie says. "It's cruel."

"This is a first. I've never been called cruel. Let me tell you what is cruel, Valerie. Cruel is constantly throwing women like Melissa and Aylin in my face. They are whores I pay dearly for. I prefer them because they are clean, unlike the women on street corners. They are nothing more to me than temporary employees. They provide a service, and I walk away with no strings when they complete their service. I don't want to hear you mention them or anything about them again. Do you understand, Ms. Richards?"

"Yes, sir," Valerie says quietly.

The ride to Ender's office is silent. Valerie looks out her window the entire trip. Finally, when they arrive, Ender gets out and waits on the sidewalk for Joseph to help Valerie out.

"I suggest you put a smile on that pretty face of yours and pretend you like me," Ender says in a harsh voice. He holds the door for Valerie, and they walk in. But, instead of giving Valerie the tour he promised, Ender gives the task to his secretary. He goes directly into his office and slams the door. The secretary delivers Valerie to Ender's office when the tour is completed.

Ender rises and walks over to a table sitting in a corner. "This, Ms. Richards, is the hotel I'm planning to build in Miami."

Valerie walks over to the table and studies the model for a long time. "How long will it take to complete?"

"Thirty-six months is the estimate if there's no hurricane. I can see your mind working, Valerie. I would like to hear your thoughts and be honest."

"Thirty-six months is a long time with no income being generated. Is there room for expansion?" Ender nods.

"Valerie, I have the model on my computer. Why don't you show me what you have in mind? We can manipulate it as we go?"

"Okay," Valerie replies and follows Ender over to his desk.

"Let me copy the file, and then you can have the computer." Ender copies the file and then steps back, allowing Valerie to sit in his chair. He pulls up a chair to sit beside her and watches as she takes control of the mouse.

Valerie explains she would build two buildings simultaneously if it were her project. One would be a smaller version of the hotel and completed first. Then, when the large hotel is completed, the smaller could be remodeled into condos and sold. That would generate income while the large hotel is being finished.

Next, Valerie explains she would build the buildings in the shape of a rhombus instead of a rectangle. She explains that, historically, hurricanes approach Miami from a particular direction. If one corner of the rhombus points in that direction, the corner would take the direct hit and help deflect some of the wind. The opposite corner of the rhombus on the smaller hotel would face the large hotel. The smaller hotel could be arranged so that corners would be closets or other spaces that didn't require windows, thus helping to cut down on construction sounds.

Ender watches as Valerie creates an entirely new model for the hotel. Her mind and her skill with the computer program fascinate him. As she works, Ender asks questions and makes notes.

"There," Valerie says. "That's just my idea. Sorry to have wasted your time, Mr. Dogan."

Ender stands and pulls Valerie to her feet. "You, my dear, should have been an architect. Your ideas are fascinating and enticing. I like the idea of generating income while building the major hotel. Do you mind if I discuss this with Murat? I promise to give you all the credit."

"I don't need the credit, Ender. I just want to make you happy with me again," Valerie says in a low voice, looking down.

Ender cups her cheek with one hand. "Valerie, look at me." She does it slowly. "Just because I get angry with you doesn't mean I'm not happy with you." His hand slides to the back of Valerie's neck while his other hand moves to the small of her back. "I'm tired of waiting for you to ask me," he whispers. He pulls her to him and kisses her.

Valerie returns the kiss, which pleases Ender. Then her arms go around his neck, and the fingers of one hand run through his hair. Ender's tongue teases Valerie's lips until she opens them and invites his tongue into her mouth. He explores every inch, first running the tip of his tongue against her teeth. When

Ender reaches her tongue, Valerie matches his rhythm and pushes her body into his.

One kiss turns into many. When Valerie pauses to catch her breath, Ender kisses every inch of her face and neck before returning to her mouth. Ender commits every sound Valerie makes to memory. As much as he wants to touch all of her, Ender consciously decides to be a gentleman and moves his hands to Valerie's hips, where he can hold her tightly against him. His body reacts to her, and Ender knows Valerie can feel it.

The buzz of the intercom interrupts the couple. Ender backs away and bends over, placing his hands on his knees to catch his breath. Valerie sits on the desk and leans back on her hands, taking deep breaths.

"Mr. Dogan, it's lunchtime. Would you like me to order something for you?" the secretary asks in Turkish.

"No, thanks. Ms. Richards and I will go out to lunch," Ender answers in English and presses the End button. "There's a private bathroom in the corner over there if you would like to freshen up."

"Thanks, I guess I should," Valerie says, sliding off the desk. "Now, aren't you glad I didn't ask?" She smiles and walks toward the bathroom.

Hell yes, I'm glad you didn't ask, Ender thinks, trying to bring his body under control. But, holy cow, that woman can kiss. He sits down in his chair. I'm feeling so many emotions now that I've never felt before. I wonder what that's about. It will be exciting to find out how much of a fireball she is in bed. But not yet, Ender decides. I'll let her take the lead since she's so hung up on the whore issue. Valerie returns from the bathroom. Ender stands and walks over to her. He takes her hand and places it on his chest, where the buttons are undone.

"Ms. Richards, if I had known having my shirt unbuttoned would turn you on, I would have done it a lot sooner," Ender states with a lopsided grin.

Valerie runs her fingertips through the hair she can reach. "I might have gotten turned on every time I saw you without a shirt," she replies, matching his grin. Ender places a gentle kiss on her lips and goes into the bathroom to comb his hair. When he returns, Valerie smiles and wipes the lipstick off his lips.

"Where are we going for lunch?" she asks.

"I know just the place, and it's within walking distance." Ender places the hand on her back and leads her out of the office to the restaurant.

Chapter 28

Valerie

Lunch was amazing, Valerie thinks after returning to the house. Ender picked a small Italian restaurant and got a table in the back. They were alone and could talk about her ideas for the hotel without interruption. Ender was attentive, holding her hand and brushing her hair back behind her ears a few times.

When he kissed me, I felt things I had never felt before with another man. It was exciting, almost forbidden. Well, he is your boss, so an inner voice says it probably should be forbidden. But, the voice continued, this will not turn out very well for you, and you know it.

Valerie lies down on the sofa and wonders if the excitement of Ender's kisses caused would carry over into bed. I'm sure he's very experienced after being with those whores. I need to move past that, but one thing's for sure. I'm not getting into bed with Ender until I know he hasn't been with them in a while.

There's a knock on her door, and Andrew pokes his head in. "Hi, Valerie. Did I catch you at a bad time?"

"No, Andrew. Please come in. I hope you brought me some work."

"As a matter of fact, I did, but first, I have to ask what you did at the office this morning? Ender and Murat have been behind closed doors all afternoon. I even heard Ender yelling at Murat, though that's not entirely unusual."

Valerie laughs and says, "I did little except look at the hotel model and give Ender my thoughts about the project."

"Good for you. Sometimes, I think Ender relies on Murat too much. Murat is a talented architect, but many out there are much better. Plus, I think Murat is a scumbag." Andrew smiles and winks.

"Well, Andrew, you and I agree on that. So what did you bring me?"

Andrew hands Valerie a folder and goes over everything with her. There are three invitations to events in Miami and four in Istanbul. "I do not know if Ender will want to attend these here in Istanbul, but I translated them for you. I also wrote out his typical Turkish responses to accept or decline. Then, after you've discussed it with him, I can translate them into Turkish and send them out."

"You are truly a wonder, Andrew. I need to talk to Ender about starting my Turkish lessons. I'm eager to get started."

"I bet you are. Well, I better go. I'm having dinner with a special friend tonight."

"Enjoy your dinner. You get little free time, and neither does Joseph, so take advantage of it," Valerie says with a smile.

"How, how did you know?" Andrew stammers.

"A woman knows these things, and what she doesn't know, she can usually figure out. So don't worry, your secret is safe with me."

About ten minutes after Andrew leaves, there's another knock on Valerie's door. She says come in, and Ender walks in with a huge smile. He walks over to her, pulls her into his arms, and kisses her deeply for several minutes.

"I've been waiting all afternoon to do that," Ender says as he kisses her neck.

"Welcome home, Mr. Dogan," Valerie moans and whispers.

"I have a lot to tell you over dinner. Why don't we go for a swim first?"

"That sounds like an excellent idea. It won't take me but a minute to change."

Ender continues to kiss her neck and whispers, "wear a bikini, please." Then he stops and leaves the room.

Ender is standing by the pool when Valerie gets there. His back is to her, and he's on the phone speaking in Turkish. She uses the time to admire his gorgeous body. He must work out, although I don't know when and he's never mentioned it. You can only get broad shoulders like that from lifting weights. Her eyes drift down to where his trunks rest below his hips. The trunks are loose around his behind, unlike the jeans Ender sometimes wears.

Valerie is lost in her thoughts about his butt in tight jeans when Ender turns around, catching her by surprise. Her eyes are pointed directly at his crotch. Valerie looks up at Ender's eyes quickly and blushes. He grins at her, says something into the phone, and hangs up.

"A penny for your thoughts, Ms. Richards," Ender says, looking Valerie up and down as he walks toward her slowly like a cat on the prowl.

"Uh, I don't think so, Mr. Dogan," Valerie replies, looking down.

Ender stands so close to Valerie that she can feel his body's heat. He leans over, kisses her cheek, and says, "I wonder if your thoughts were as inappropriate as mine were when I saw you just now?"

"Maybe or maybe not, Ender."

"Share your thoughts, and I'll share mine."

"Nice girls don't tell things like that," Valerie says, smiling timidly.

"Well, if you don't want to talk about it, then why don't you show me instead," Ender whispers, gently nipping her earlobe but not touching her with his hands.

"Ender, the cameras."

"I turned them off, hoping you might want to live dangerously out here."

"No, you didn't," Valerie moans as Ender continues nibbling on her ear.

"You're right. I didn't, but one can always hope," he says, backing away and diving into the pool.

Valerie watches the perfect strokes of the handsome man as his body cuts through the water. Ender doesn't stop until he's made five laps around the pool. "Aren't you coming in?" he asks, leaning against the pool, brushing the water from his face. Valerie nods and dives in. She swims two laps until she feels hands around her waist, lifting her.

"You are so small and delicate," Ender says when Valerie's head breaks the water. "I bet you're a tigress in bed, though."

"I've been called worse," Valerie says, blushing.

"You just didn't have the right man. I can't wait to share my bed with you." Ender looks deeply into her eyes. She can see his desire for her in them. "I have decided that there will be no other women in my life. I will wait for you."

Chapter 29

Ender

Where the hell did that, come from a voice inside Ender's mind asks? He releases Valerie and swims away without waiting for her to comment. As he swims, a second voice appears inside his head. You told her that because it's true. You don't want her to worry about other women; you aren't interested in being with anyone else.

What is happening to me, Ender wonders? Since kissing Valerie this morning, I've had strange thoughts and feelings, and now I'm hearing voices. I'm even considering her feelings when I've considered no one's but my own. I better call my therapist tomorrow and see how fast I can get to see him. If I'm going crazy, maybe he can give me something to stop it. When Ender finally grows tired, he climbs out of the pool to find he's alone. He dries off and heads inside to get ready for dinner.

Ender is sitting at the dining table when Valerie appears carrying her tote. As she sits the tote in the chair next to hers, Ender takes time to admire her choice of casual wear for dinner. Valerie is wearing a pink off-the-shoulder crop top that stresses her shoulders and flat stomach. Her shorts are white and shorter than usual. Ender feels his body react and shifts in his seat.

He clears his throat and says, "let's discuss your items first, and then I'll tell you my news." Ender declines all the new invitations from Istanbul. "Tomorrow is Thursday, and I'll finish my business here. We'll fly back to Miami on Friday, so let's wait to discuss any Miami invitations until we get there. I know it's a week earlier than I originally planned. Does that mess up any plans you have, Valerie?"

"No, Ender. That sounds fine. When we get back, can we discuss beginning my Turkish lessons? I'm eager to get started."

"Of course. Now, are you ready to hear my news?" Ender says excitedly. Valerie nods. "Let's go into the living area." He leads the way, sits on the sofa, and pulls her into his lap. "That's much better," Ender says, nuzzling her neck.

"Tell me your news," Valerie says.

"Okay, okay. First, I discussed your ideas with Murat. It offended him I liked your ideas and refused to redo his drawings. So I fired him from the project and gave him a smaller one."

"Oh, no, Ender. I was only sharing my thoughts with you. I never thought you would take me seriously," Valerie says, shocked.

"Valerie, they were brilliant suggestions and made great sense. Murat should have thought of some of those things. That's what he gets paid to do."

"I bet Murat wasn't happy."

"No, but his new project will keep him in Turkey. Murat hasn't been keeping a low profile as far as women are concerned. It is causing problems with his wife. He needs to get his act together, or he will support an ex-wife."

"Ender, this will delay your project."

"I've got it under control. I talked to the project manager I hired. He will contact three architects he's worked with in the past. If they are interested, I want to talk to them next week. This won't delay the project much because we are still getting building permits and other things from Miami officials."

Valerie looks away from Ender. "I'm sorry, Ender. It's all my fault."

"Let me show you what is your fault." Ender pushes Valerie down on the sofa and pins her with his body. "It's your fault that I want to kiss you over and over and over again." He leans down and starts with a tender kiss that becomes more passionate as Valerie responds.

After several minutes of intense kissing, Ender stops and looks down at Valerie. "As much as I want you, I'll wait until you're ready."

"Thank you, Ender," Valerie whispers.

"I have work to do. I'll see you in the morning." Ender gets up and leaves the room.

Ha, work! Work in the bathroom, one voice in his head says. Leave him alone, the other voice says. You're just confusing him. No, the first voice says. Valerie's confusing him.

Later, unable to sleep, Ender moves to the living area and sits on an ottoman with his head in his hands. Minutes later, two dainty hands are placed on his shoulders, and a soft kiss is placed on the back of his neck.

"Ender, it's late. You should be in bed," Valerie whispers against his neck.

He places his hands on top of hers. "I can't sleep. My mind won't stop turning."

"Do you want to talk about it?"

"No, I'm just having difficulty gathering my thoughts together."

"Do you need to go see Aylin?"

"No, Valerie. Seeing her is the last thing I want to do." Ender moves his hands to his face and rubs his eyes.

Valerie moves to stand in front of him. "Ender, come to bed with me."

"No. Valerie, you aren't ready for that yet." He looks into her eyes and sees what appears to be a tender look.

"I'm not suggesting that, Ender. Just come lie down with me and let me hold you." She offers him her hand. Ender takes it and follows her upstairs to her bedroom. Valerie lies down, and he lies down beside her. She moves his head to lie on her chest as she wraps her arms around him. Ender falls into a deep, relaxed slumber in minutes.

Chapter 30

Ender

E nder wakes at 7:00 am. He is still lying in Valerie's arms. He deeply inhales her jasmine scent and then eases away from her to sit on the side of the bed. Wow, I slept like a baby in her arms. Maybe I should do this more often. He smiles. Ender walks downstairs to his office and writes Valerie a note apologizing for leaving early, but he will see her tonight. Next, he goes into the garden and cuts a stem of blooming jasmine. Finally, Ender goes back upstairs, pleased to see Valerie still sleeping. He leaves the note and the jasmine on the pillow next to her.

"Well, Ender, I must say it surprised me to hear from you this morning. It's been over a year since you were here last," the therapist says. "Tell me what's going on for you to book an appointment for three hours."

"It's the woman. No, it's me. No, it's everything, and I don't understand any of it," Enders states.

"Are you talking about the woman we discussed a year ago? The one you couldn't forget?" Ender nods. "Well, tell me about her."

Ender tells the therapist about running into Valerie at the sidewalk café and finding out she worked for the firm he bought. Then, he described hiring her as his assistant.

"Well, Ender, that is quite a story. Small world, isn't it?" the therapist asks with a smile, not expecting an answer. "So, what's the problem?"

"Valerie, that's her name, is making me crazy. You know me. I don't care about anyone's feelings but my own. Suddenly, I'm thinking about what she might want to do, to eat, where to go, etc."

"Ender, have you and Valerie become intimate?"

"No, and that's weird, too. We tease each other, but I didn't kiss her for the first time until yesterday. I decided to let her choose when she's ready to take the relationship further. We made out on the sofa last night, and I was a perfect gentleman."

"Are you still seeing your whores regularly?"

"It seems I've lost interest in that. I never gave up my women while I was married. Valerie knows about the whores. I can tell it bothers her, so I told her I wouldn't be with one while I'm waiting for her. The words just came out of my mouth."

"Okay, what else?"

"I can't sleep. I have all these feelings and emotions I can't describe. Sometimes it's hard to concentrate on my work. I want to be with Valerie all the time. Last night, she found me awake in the living area and asked me to sleep with her. Just sleep. She held me in her arms, and I went to sleep quickly and slept like a child. It felt calming to be there."

The therapist observes Ender. He can't sit still. He's constantly wringing his hands or running his fingers through his hair. Finally, after several minutes, the therapist says, "Ender, I think I know what the problem is, and I think you know but don't want to admit it to yourself."

Ender looks over at the man and says, "well, what is it? Are you going to tell me or leave it to me to figure it out?"

"Hmmm. Let's go review something first that you told me before." The therapist flips back through his notepad, looking for a particular note he wrote. "Ah, here it is. You said you've never been in love. You didn't want to be in a relationship with anyone because there was no such thing as a long-term, honest relationship. Also, you said you are extremely selfish and didn't want to share anything with anyone else. Isn't that what you told me?"

"Yes, I said all those things the first time we met. So what?" Ender replies.

"Let's start with the last statement. Didn't you say earlier that now you are considering what Valerie wants?" Ender nods. "That doesn't sound very selfish, and you're sharing your personal space with her now, even though she's your employee. But, of course, that's not selfish either, considering it was your idea."

"It was a perk to hire her, is all," Ender says.

"If you say so, Ender. Next, you've never been in love but are having these feelings and emotions, you say, that are new for you. Would you say these feelings are good feelings and emotions, and how do they make you feel?"

Ender takes several minutes to decide the answer. Finally, he speaks. "Well, I feel warm and happy when I have these feelings and emotions. I guess you could say content and almost carefree. They feel natural somehow, even though I haven't felt them before."

"When do you experience these feelings and emotions the most?"

"I seem only to have them when I'm with Valerie. Why?"

"Could you be having feelings for Valerie?" the therapist asks.

"You mean like I'm falling for her? That's funny," Ender scoffs.

"Is it, Ender?"

"Of course it is. I'm not one of those men that falls for a beautiful woman with a kind heart. A woman whose eyes have amber flecks sparking from them when she's angry. A woman who can tease and make me laugh and who can kiss like no one has ever kissed me before."

"Ender, I think you just answered your own question. Now our time is up. You told me on the phone you're going to Miami tomorrow. Consider what we've talked about. We can always do a video call if you want to do any future sessions. I think, under the circumstances, at least one more session would be good."

Burak drops Ender off at the office after lunch. The project manager has emailed Ender the names of three architects for the hotel project. Ender spends the rest of the day researching the architects and viewing their social media pages. The afternoon goes by quickly. Ender doesn't realize how late it is until his secretary knocks on the door to tell him she's leaving for the day.

As Ender packs up items to take home and review, his mind wanders to Valerie, and he can't wait to see her and have dinner with her.

Chapter 31

Valerie

Valerie yawns before diving into the warm water of the pool. I got little sleep because I was holding Ender, she thinks. But, at least, he went to sleep and wasn't restless. That was sweet of him to leave the note and jasmine next to me this morning. That's a first for him.

While she swims, Valerie makes a mental note to ask Ender what time they are leaving for Miami tomorrow. Joseph didn't know when she asked him this morning. I hate to leave sooner than planned because there are so many things I want to see, but maybe next trip. Valerie senses she is being watched and breaks the water's surface before reaching the pool's edge.

Ender sits at the edge with his bare legs dangling in the water. He grins at her and says, "hi, beautiful."

"Hi, yourself," Valerie says, reaching under the water to tickle the bottom of his feet.

"Lady, you shouldn't have done that," Ender says sternly. He slides down into the pool and goes under the water. Valerie looks around and feels Ender's arm snake around her waist from behind. She tries to swim away, but his grip is tight.

Ender tickles her sides with his free hand, making Valerie giggle and struggle to get away. Suddenly, the top of her bikini comes untied because Valerie squirms and floats away. Ender notices the top at the same time as Valerie, and they watch it as if in slow motion. As he turns to grab for the top and his arm around Valerie's waist slides up underneath her breasts. Ender quickly releases her and swims away, retrieving the top.

"Here, put this back on," he says as he hands her the top and turns his back.

A very disappointed Valerie takes the top, turns her back to Ender, and puts the top back on. She then dives under the water to hide the tears in her eyes. Valerie swims three laps and then climbs out of the pool.

Ender is sitting at the edge of a chaise. "I'm sorry about that, Valerie."

She grabs a towel and mutters, "it's okay. I'm going to get ready for dinner." She turns to walk away, but Ender is quickly there beside her.

He lifts her chin, forcing her to look at him. "Valerie, I will not touch you until you're ready. I can only hope it will be soon because I want you so badly." She nods and walks away.

Valerie pulls off the bikini in her room, lies on the bed, and cries. I want Ender just as badly, if not more than he says he wants me. But I need to be sure I'm the only woman he's with when he does. It's not that I'm afraid of catching anything. On the contrary, I want him to feel something for me and be the only woman on his mind. At this point, I'm willing to lose my job to have one night with him. I hope when that time comes, I won't disappoint him.

Finally, she climbs off the bed, showers, and dresses for dinner in jeans and a polo shirt. Although she applied makeup, Valerie cannot disguise her puffy red eyes. She grabs her tote and heads downstairs to find Ender waiting for her.

"You've been crying," he says, taking her into his arm. "Am I the cause of your tears?" he whispers in her ears.

"No, Ender. It's me and my indecisions and my insecurities."

"I'm not trying to pressure you," he replies.

"I know, and I appreciate that. You are just so experienced, and I'm not. It's intimidating to think about."

Ender takes the tote from her hand and sets it on the floor. He lifts her, carrying her to the living area. He sits down with her in his lap. "Valerie, look at me, please." She does as tears of embarrassment fill her eyes. "What I'm experienced in is nothing like what I want to experience with you. Your pleasure will be my pleasure. I want to hear you scream my name in passion. I want to kiss and learn every inch of your body. I want to satisfy you as no other man has before me."

Now the tears run down Valerie's cheeks. Ender kisses them away, then kisses her lips. Valerie puts her arms around his neck, pulling him closer to her. She feels her body respond with a vengeance to Ender's deep kisses. Valerie also knows Ender's body reacts to her.

"I want to hear you call my name as well," Valerie whispers.

"There's no doubt in my mind that you can make that happen, baby," Ender whispers back. "Now we better go have dinner before I can't stop myself, even though I said I would." He lifts Valerie. She watches as he adjusts himself and licks her lips. When she looks up, Ender winks at her.

Valerie goes over her short list of invitations during dinner, all of which are for Istanbul. Since they are going back to Miami tomorrow, Ender declines all of them.

"Valerie, wasn't there an event on Saturday night in Miami?" Ender asks.

She looks through her planner. "Yes, it is a fundraiser for the mayor's re-election."

"Okay, email them to ask if it's too late to attend. If it is still open, respond that I'll attend with a date. What time does it start?"

"7:30, and it's black tie," Valerie responds.

"Great. That should give you enough time to get your hair and makeup done. Since you won't have time to buy a new dress, take the cream-colored gown with the gold threads back to Miami with us."

"Uh, Ender, you want me to be your date?"

"Yes, I do. Is that a problem?" Ender reaches across the table and takes her hand.

"No. No problem whatsoever. I'm just surprised, is all," Valerie responds.

"Yes, it is a part of your job, but not that night. I want you to be my date, not my employee." Ender thinks for a few seconds. "Wait. I messed that up. Since I want you to go as my date, I need to rephrase that." He clears his throat. "Valerie, would you go to the fundraiser as my date Saturday night?"

"I would enjoy that very much, Ender. Thank you for asking," Valerie smiles. "Now, what time are we leaving tomorrow?"

"I think we will leave at 11:00 am. Andrew is already on a plane, so I better ask Joseph to let the pilot know. What would you like to do this evening?"

"Ender, since it is our last night here for a while, I would like to take a walk through the garden before it gets dark. Will you walk with me?"

"I would love to. Give me five minutes to send a couple of messages. Then, I'll meet you on the patio." Valerie nods, loads her tote and carries it upstairs.

Oh, my gosh! Ender actually asked me to go to the fundraiser as his date. Maybe, just maybe, I'm making a little progress with him. Plus, he has come home after work every night. I'm going to hope that's a good sign.

Chapter 32

Ender

After a long stroll through the garden, Ender stops at the bench where he found Valerie passed out a few nights earlier. He sits down and pulls her into his lap. The couple spends several minutes kissing before Ender forces himself to stop.

"Valerie, can I sleep with you again tonight? I slept so well last night next to you."

"Of course, but it's your turn to hold me," Valerie says shyly.

"It will be a sacrifice for me, but I'll try," Ender replies with a grin. Valerie pokes him in the ribs, stands, and offers him her hand. Ender takes it and stands beside her, pulling her into his arms. "We'll be back here in a month or two. It will be cooler then, so let's do another walk-through if you don't mind."

"I would like that," Valerie says, "as long as you hold my hand."

Back inside the house, Ender goes to his bedroom, and Valerie goes to hers. Ender looks at his bed and texts Valerie. "Come sleep in my bed tonight." He receives no response and is retyping the text when there's a knock on his door. Ender goes to the door and there stands Valerie.

"I got your message," she grins.

"I was beginning to think you didn't, or you changed your mind because you didn't answer. Come in. I was about to change." When Ender returns from his closet, Valerie is already in bed. He climbs in beside her and pulls her into his arms. They kiss several times and then settle in for the night.

Ender watches Valerie as she sleeps and thinks about what he and the therapist discussed this morning. I admit; I feel so content and happy when I'm with Valerie. Lying here in bed with her feels like this is how life should be. But am I falling for her? I hope not. I'm not the right man for her and never will be.

When the plane takes off, it is only Ender, Valerie, and Joseph on board. All three sit with seats between them so they can spread out and work. Joseph sits near the front, Valerie in the middle, and Ender in the back.

Two hours outside Istanbul, Ender says, "Joseph. I have a few things for you to do when we get back." Joseph walks to the middle of the plane so he can hear better. "First, I want you to work with Andrew to find a full-time tutor for Valerie to teach her Turkish, that can live in one apartment. Second, I want you to hire two additional security guards. Finally, it's time for you to take on more of a supervisor role so you can move into one apartment."

"Okay, but you want two additional security officers, and there are no vacant apartments."

"That's correct. Valerie will move upstairs to the large vacant bedroom. You can move into hers since it is the largest. Burak can have the last vacant apartment. The two new men can share the suite you and Burak are currently in."

A message pops up on Ender's phone. He looks down and sees it's from Valerie. "*Are you sure you want that?*" the message says. "*I'm 100% sure.*" Ender types out his reply and sends it.

"Yes, sir. I'll start working on it right now. Will there be anything else?" Joseph asks.

"No, that's all," Ender replies.

Chapter 33

Valerie

After lunch, Ender retires to the large bedroom for a nap. Joseph waits for several minutes and sits next to Valerie.

"Are you okay moving upstairs with Ender?" he asks in a low voice.

"I guess I have to since the decision was made for me. Do you have concerns, Joseph?"

"Ender can be mean and vindictive one minute and sweet as sugar the next. I don't want to see you hurt. That's my concern."

"I can take care of myself."

"Okay. Do you still have that card I gave you?" Valerie nods yes. "Good. Your phone is tracked and monitored now, which means Ender can see all incoming and outgoing calls and messages."

"I have nothing to hide, Joseph."

"Not now, but the day may come when you will. Once I get back to Miami, I will get burner phones for us. You can contact my brother or me if you need help. Because of the security cameras, you and I can't talk freely in the apartment. The cars are off limits, too."

"Joseph, is that really necessary?"

"Valerie, I've known Ender long, and I believe it is for your sake. I think you know you can trust me, and I trust you. I'll find a way to get the phone to you without Ender's knowledge. Hide it somewhere so only you know where it is. If you're not near the phone and I will send you a message, I'll signal you by pulling on my right earlobe. Take care of yourself and be safe." Joseph stands and starts to walk back to his seat.

"What were the two of you talking about?" Ender asks, returning to his seat in the back.

Valerie stands and walks toward him. "Joseph is already trying to find me a tutor. He asked if I preferred a male tutor or a female tutor. I told him it didn't make any difference to me." Ender nods, and Valerie walks past him, heading to the bathroom.

At the Miami apartment, Valerie pushes the button for her floor after entering the elevator. "Valerie, all your things have been moved upstairs, so there's no reason to stop at that floor. Joseph, would you turn off the security cameras in the penthouse? No one knows we're back yet. I'll let you know when to turn them back on."

"Yes, sir," Joseph replies.

When they step off the elevator at the penthouse, Joseph heads back to turn the cameras off, leaving Ender and Valerie alone. Ender reaches for Valerie, but she backs away. She looks up at him with the amber flecks growing exponentially.

"Is this the way it's going to be?" Valerie asks.

"What?" Ender replies.

"Deciding for me without talking to me first?"

"What decisions?"

"What dress to wear to an event? Where will I live? Moving my stuff?" Valerie says with fire in her eyes.

"Okay, I should have discussed things with you first, but here's how I look at it. First, I'm familiar with the events I choose to attend and what women typically wear to those events. Second, I selected or had someone select your gowns based on my knowledge. Third, I thought if we were going to sleep together, it would be easier for you to be in the same living space so we wouldn't attract gossip or speculation. Finally, I thought I was doing you a favor by having your stuff moved for you since we got here late." Ender takes a deep breath. "If you want to be angry with me, that's your business, but please, don't flash those amber flecks at me when I want you so badly."

Valerie looks down at the floor. "I'm sorry. I just wish we had talked about things first."

"And I'm sorry I didn't. I'll try to do better. Now, I'm going to bed. Hopefully, you'll join me so I can sleep." Ender turns and walks toward his bedroom.

Valerie takes a quick shower in her new bedroom and changes into her pajamas. By the time she reaches Ender's bedroom, he's sleeping. She carefully climbs into bed, turns away from him, and backs up to him. Ender puts his arm across her waist and snuggles closer.

Chapter 34

Valerie

After breakfast, Valerie walks around her new suite, deciding where to place the meager personal items she brought with her when she moved. Time goes by quickly, and the stylist arrives at 3:00 pm. Valerie dresses and is in the living area when Ender walks in his tux.

"Will you straighten my tie?" he asks as he walks toward Valerie. "You look gorgeous. Let's stay here. I don't feel like getting into a fight tonight."

"Why would you get into a fight?" Valerie asks, straightening his tie.

"All the men there will want to hold you and do this." Ender places his hands on her hips and pulls Valerie to him. He kisses one side of her neck and shoulders and then moves to the other side.

This must be what a hot flash feels like; only this is one thousand times hotter, Valerie thinks as Ender's lips glide over her. I can't take much more of this. I'll see how tonight goes.

"You're breathing hard," Ender whispers in her ear. "I bet your whole body craves to be kissed like this."

"You're not being fair, Ender," Valerie moans. "I don't know how to make you feel the things you make me feel."

"You don't have to know how. With you, it comes with a greater force than a nuclear bomb. My whole body aches for you whenever I see, smell, and touch you. I don't know how much longer I can wait for you to be mine and only mine." Ender steps back. "You do not know the power you have over me." He closes his eyes and sighs. "Maybe I shouldn't have said that, but it's true. Let's go. We don't want to be late." He kisses her softly on the lips before placing his hand on her back and guiding her toward the elevator.

The night was perfect, Valerie decides on the ride back to the condo. Ender was always at her side. He introduced her as his date until Melissa walked up with another very handsome man older than Ender. Then, Ender introduced Valerie as his girlfriend to Melissa, who had a shocked look on her face for several seconds. Not as shocked as me, though, Valerie thinks. A feather could have knocked me over.

"Ender, will you unzip me?" Valerie asks when they enter the foyer of the penthouse.

"Of course," he replies as she turns around. His fingers slide over her shoulder blades to the zipper. As he slowly unzips the dress, Valerie can feel his breath on her back. "All done," Ender whispers in her ear.

Valerie turns around slowly, holding her dress up with both hands, and looks into his eyes. She sees them darken with desire. Desire for her and only her. Valerie lets go of the dress, letting it fall into a pile at her feet. She watches as Ender's eyes slide down her body, taking in the skimpy white lacy of her lingerie.

His eyes return to hers, and he says, "are you sure?" Valerie smiles and nods. Ender lifts her and carries her to his bedroom. He sets her down beside the bed and turns the bedcovers back. Next, he takes his time undressing her, letting his hands slide over her body as he removes every piece of lingerie. Then, he lifts her, lying her down in the center of the bed.

Chapter 35

Ender

He walks to the edge of the bed and gazes at the most beautiful woman he's ever seen. "Are you sure, Valerie? We can stop now if you want to."

"Please, Ender. Make me yours," Valerie says, staring into his eyes.

Ender takes his time undressing. His eyes never leaving hers. Finally, he slowly climbs onto the bed, takes her into him, and kisses her with more passion than he has ever felt in his life.

Several hours later, Ender lies on his back with Valerie's head on his shoulder. She is running her fingers through the hair on his chest.

"I dreamed about what your chest would feel like when I touched it," she says.

"Is it better or worse?"

"It's better, so much better." Valerie yawns.

"Are you sleepy?" Valerie nods. "That's too bad because I'm not finished with you yet," Ender says, turning to kiss her.

The sky is turning pink with the sunrise when Ender finally lets Valerie sleep. He's tired, but he marvels at the woman beside him. Her energy matched his, and that's saying a lot because he couldn't get enough of Valerie. The feelings and emotions I felt while making love to her were foreign to me, but so very nice, he thinks. Maybe I am falling for her. She's already changed my life in many ways. I think about some things differently now. The funny thing is that it doesn't scare me. It calms me, and I feel I have a purpose other than my business. I'll have to see how this goes. Ender closes his eyes and falls into a dreamless sleep.

Something is tickling Ender's belly, waking him. He looks down to see it's Valerie's hair. Oh, she's just lying there sleeping. Uh no, she's not sleeping, he quickly decides as his body reacts to her mouth and hands. He closes his eyes, clenches his fists, and enjoys every minute of Valerie's hair moving across his stomach.

"Can we stay in bed today?" Valerie asks as she moves up Ender's body to lie in his arms.

"I think I'm going to have to. I don't think I can move," Ender answers, grinning at her. "We need to eat eventually, though. But, unfortunately, we don't have room service here."

"I'm getting hungry. I'll go fix something," Valerie says. She kisses his cheek, climbs off the bed, and puts his shirt on, causing Ender to laugh. "What so funny?"

"You're so short that shirt hits you below the knees, hiding your gorgeous legs. Put that lingerie back on instead."

"What if Joseph or Burak walk into the kitchen?"

"They won't. I texted them earlier and gave them the day off. I told them not to disturb us for any reason." As Ender watches, Valerie drops the shirt and puts on the lingerie he took off last night. "Much better," he remarks. "Now, you better hurry and get out of here because I'm feeling frisky all over again." Valerie giggles and runs from the room.

When Ender steps out of the shower, he smells bacon. He smiles and says, thank goodness I don't practice the religion I was raised in. I love my bacon. He wraps a towel around his waist and heads to the kitchen but stops in the doorway. He watches Valerie dressed in her lingerie, cooking. She looks so cute dancing around, trying to avoid the bacon splattering her skin. There's a lot of bare skin too.

Valerie looks up and sees Ender watching her. "Is that what you're wearing to brunch?"

"I want to undress quickly after brunch. I think you have too much on," Ender states, walking to her like a panther on the prowl. "Are you finished with the bacon?" Valerie nods. Ender reaches up and unhooks her bra. "There, that's so much better. Now, let's eat. I worked up an appetite last night and intend to again today."

Leaving the dirty dishes on the dining table and cabinets, as well as the lacy bra on the kitchen floor, Ender carries Valerie back to bed. They spend the rest of the day and all night in bed except to raid the fridge for food around dinnertime.

"Valerie, baby. I have to get up now," Ender says, kissing Valerie's neck.

"Do you have to get up right now?" she asks, snuggling against him.

"I could probably wait thirty minutes. What do you have in mind?"

"Let me show you," Valerie replies, crawling under the covers.

"Now, I really have to get up," Ender says an hour and a half later. "I'm interviewing architects today. So I want you to do something fun today."

"Fun? Like what?"

"Go shopping for more lingerie," Ender answers with a huge grin, raising his eyebrows up and down.

"Why? You don't leave it on long enough to appreciate it?" Valerie asks.

"That's true, but taking it off is so much fun."

Chapter 36

Valerie

After Ender leaves, Valerie showers and dresses. She sits on the bed, reliving Saturday night and all day Sunday. Ender was so gentle about making love to her. He was only concerned about her and how she felt the entire time. I could get used to being with him, and I'm falling for him. I'm falling hard. She gets up, goes back into the bathroom, and begins digging around in her makeup bag. Dammit, I left my birth control pills in Istanbul. I haven't had one since Friday morning. Well, two days won't matter. I'll call the doctor and get a refill when I return from shopping.

Over the next two months, the pair falls into a routine. On weekdays, Ender gets up in the mornings and goes to the office. Valerie works with her tutor, learning the Turkish language. Ender gets home from work between 5:30 and 6:00. They have dinner together and discuss event invitations. After dinner, Ender and Valerie watch TV, work, or play games until bedtime, when the fun begins. On the weekends, they visit tourist attractions around Miami, go to the beach, or attend formal events. Every minute Ender isn't at work is spent with Valerie.

At the end of the second month, the pair is lying in bed. "Valerie, I was cleaning up my office today and came across your personnel file," Ender says. "I guess I never returned it to HR. Anyway, I was reading through it and the notes I made after your interview."

"Okay, is there a problem?" Valerie asks.

"No, but I have a question. When I asked where you saw yourself in five years, I got a fairly standard professional answer, but nothing personal."

"What do you want to know now that you couldn't legally ask then?" Valerie laughs, turning to face Ender.

"Well, do you hope to get married someday?"

"I don't know. If I love someone and want to share my life with him, I don't feel I have to marry him. What about you? Do you think you'll ever remarry?"

"No, I can't see myself committing to one woman. I don't know what love is, so I wouldn't know how to show it or receive it. So a long-term relationship is out of the question for me. Besides, I already told you how I feel about kids."

"So you don't consider what we are doing in a relationship?" Valerie asks, turning over on her back to stare at the ceiling.

"It is partly a business relationship and the rest of fun. Now, speaking of fun, let's have some."

"I don't think so tonight, Ender. My stomach's been queasy all day. If I have a stomach bug, I don't want you to get it. So let's just go to sleep. Hopefully, I'll feel better in the morning."

"Okay. I noticed you hardly ate anything at dinner." Ender rises on his elbow and kisses her cheek. "Goodnight, Valerie."

Valerie turns away from Ender and silently cries. Ender might be attentive and a little more considerate than he was initially, but he has no feelings for me. He just admitted it, and he will not change. So why did I have to fall for him? She carefully climbs out of bed.

"Where are you going?" Ender asks.

"To get some juice. I'll be back in a little while."

"Okay, baby."

"I wish you wouldn't call me that," Valerie says, walking out of the room. Valerie gets a glass of apple juice and goes to the living area. Even though it is a warm night in Miami, Valerie turns on the fireplace and watches the fire. Finally, her eyes get heavy, and she lies on the sofa.

When she wakes the following day, Valerie is still on the sofa. The fireplace has been turned off. The clock on the mantle reads 9:00 am. She gets up and goes to the kitchen, looking for Ender. Instead, the housekeeper tells Valerie he left an hour ago. Valerie refuses breakfast because her stomach is still queasy.

As she steps into the shower, Valerie thinks it's odd Ender didn't carry her to bed, nor did he tell her goodbye. However, her thoughts are cut short when she gags and throws up. Feeling hot, Valerie leans against the shower wall. "Please don't let me be pregnant," she whispers aloud.

Valerie finishes her shower, dresses, and texts Joseph that she needs to run an errand. I'll buy a pregnancy test and pray that it's negative. Joseph drives Valerie to a pharmacy, where she uses her personal credit card and buys five pregnancy tests.

Returning home, Valerie rushes to her bedroom and uses all five pregnancy tests. She paces the bedroom, waiting for the results. Finally, it is time to look at the results. All five tests show positive. "Dammit," she says aloud. "What am I going to do? Ender doesn't like kids and doesn't want any. I need to think before I say anything to him and act as if nothing is going on."

That night, Ender returns home at his usual time. However, he doesn't greet Valerie with a hug and kiss like usual. He doesn't ask her how she feels. To Valerie, it seems the past two months have been erased from Ender's memory. Instead, he treats her the way he did right after hiring her.

After their dinner and the nightly event invitations work is finished, Ender heads to his office, where he stays until bedtime.

"Ender," Valerie says, walking into his bedroom, "where would you like me to sleep tonight?"

"In here, of course. You know I sleep better with you beside me. Why are you asking me that?"

"You've practically ignored me all night. You didn't say goodbye this morning. I wasn't sure what you wanted me to do," Valerie replies.

"I have a lot on my mind. You can sleep wherever you want." Ender climbs into bed and turns away from her. Valerie gets into the bed on her side and turns away from him.

Chapter 37

Ender

Ender feels Valerie climb into bed, but he doesn't turn over. The question she asked him last night has been bothering him last night and today. She had asked if he didn't consider what they were doing as a relationship. He had replied that it was partly business and partly fun. But was that an accurate answer? In truth, it was only business during dinner when he and Valerie talked about invitations. The rest of the time, it was fun. She was fun to be around, and Ender enjoyed her company. They had a good time together, and bedtime was the best.

He was honest when he said he didn't think he could commit to one woman, but could he? After all, Valerie has been the only woman in his life for the last three months. He hadn't missed the whores at all. If I'm honest with myself, I can't wait to get home and see her. I can't wait for the weekends to come around so we can get out and do things together. I love holding her tiny hand in mine as we walk around.

Ender turns slightly and looks over his shoulder at Valerie, but she's turned away. I enjoy touching her and making love to her. Hell, I like everything about her; he decides. I'm surprised I haven't tired of her yet. The feelings and emotions I have, whatever they are, seem to get stronger. I wish I understood those feelings better. Maybe I am falling for her. Perhaps I should talk to her about it, but it could go two ways. Either she would leave me or tell me she has feelings, too. What would I do then? I don't want her to leave me, at least not yet.

Valerie said she wished he wouldn't call her baby. That was weird. He's called her that more lately than he has called her by name. Ender reaches for his phone and searches the internet for the word, baby. He reads several descriptions. Baby is often used as a term of endearment, Ender reads. Hmm, I was just using it as a nickname for her, or was I? I've never called another woman baby. I'm just so damn confused. Ender turns over and snuggles against Valerie's back. She's warm, soft, and smells good. He starts to wake her and decides against it. This makes the second straight night of not making love. They always make love before going to sleep. I don't like this one bit. I'll do better tomorrow.

Chapter 38

Valerie

When Ender snuggles up to Valerie's back, she can't help but move closer to him. The end is coming soon, she thinks. If I inform him I'm pregnant, he will insist I end the pregnancy and kick me out because I forgot about my pills. If I tell him I wish to keep the baby, he'll kick me out, accusing me of wanting his money and tricking him into marriage. I messed my life up either way. Maybe I could end the pregnancy without him ever knowing. Oh, Ender, Valerie whispers; if only you cared about me, then perhaps we could work this out together.

Early the following day, Ender is back to his usual self. He wakes Valerie and makes love to her before leaving for work. But this time is different. Ender is more passionate and caring than usual. Valerie enjoys it immensely, but it also confuses her.

After Ender leaves, Valerie decides to talk to the only person she has as a friend, Joseph. So she gets the burner phone and sends the message, "*I need to talk privately.*"

Joseph responds, "*Let's go for a walk in a park. Pick you up in ten minutes.*"

Valerie and Joseph do not talk on the drive to a park on the opposite side of town. Instead, they walk several feet away from the car and sit on a bench.

"You're pregnant, aren't you?" Joseph asks.

"How did you know?"

"Well, having grown up with older sisters, it was easy for me to figure out. You've put on a little weight, your face is slightly fuller, and you aren't eating much."

"Good gosh! If you noticed all that, I'm surprised Ender hasn't," Valerie states.

"I doubt Ender has ever been around a pregnant woman. Have you told him?"

"No, and I'm not sure I will. I have messed up my life and my job. Ender doesn't want kids and said he doesn't like them. If I tell him, I'm sure he'll insist on getting rid of the baby, and then he'll fire me. I want to keep the baby so I know he'll fire me. So I may get rid of it and not tell him at all."

"Valerie, I can't tell you what to do. You have to decide, and I'll help you in any way I can."

"Thanks, Joseph. If I decide to end the pregnancy, are there any clinics I can go to? I'll need to do something quickly."

"I'll check with my brother. Obviously, you don't want to go to one close to the apartment. I'll let you know on the burner phone when I find out. Now, would you like some time alone?" Valerie nods. Joseph goes and sits in the car and watches her closely.

Valerie sits on the bench for a very long time. She cries, not about the pregnancy, but about losing the man she has fallen in love with. Her burner phone pings with a message from Joseph's brother. The message contains a clinic name, address, and phone number. Unfortunately, the clinic isn't in the best part of Miami.

Valerie spends the next week considering all her options. Even though it is hard, she pretends everything is normal around Ender. He is back to his old self, which makes Valerie relax. They spend a wonderful weekend together on a quick trip to Orlando.

At the beginning of the next week, Valerie called the clinic to schedule an appointment. The clinic is busy, so the appointment is scheduled for Tuesday in two weeks, which is ideal. Ender leaves at noon that day for Istanbul and will return on Saturday. She should be well enough to make Ender happy in bed by then. When Ender teases her about gaining a little weight, Valerie tells him it is the excellent cooking of the housekeeper causing it.

After Ender leaves the following morning, Valerie messages Joseph on the burner phone, and they run errands. Then, finally, they return to the park to talk.

"Joseph, I've decided to end the pregnancy and not tell Ender about it."

"Valerie, are you sure that's what you want to do?"

"I really don't have any other choice. My appointment is at 1:00 pm after Ender leaves for Istanbul."

"Okay," Joseph says. "I'm not going with Ender because I need to do a few security checks on the system at the apartment. I'll suggest he take one of the new guys so Burak can take you. I'm going to ask for the rest of this week off. I need to take care of some personal business. Do you need anything before I take off?"

"No, thank you. Joseph, I know this is hard for you, keeping my secret from Ender. You are a wonderful friend."

Chapter 39

Valerie

The day of the appointment at the clinic arrives quickly. Ender spends all morning with Valerie before heading to the airport. Once he leaves at noon, Valerie messages Burak to pick her up. She gives Burak an address one block away and around the corner from the clinic, so he won't know where she is going.

Valerie enters the clinic, checks in, and provides the mandatory urine sample to verify her pregnancy. After several minutes, she is escorted to a room and given a gown to change into. Valerie clasps the gown to her chest and looks around the room. She places her hand on her belly and feels the bump inside her. She paces the room. I am choosing between my baby and Ender. I'm deciding between my baby's life and his. I can't do this.

Valerie rushes out of the room and leaves the clinic, crying. She hurries toward the car, not paying attention to the two men following her. Burak gets out of the car to open her door. Suddenly, one man knocks Valerie to the ground and grabs her purse. The other man shoots Burak as he tries to help Valerie. Both men jump into the car and speed off.

Chapter 40

Ender

Ender's noon flight out of Miami is delayed because of a storm twenty-five miles out in the ocean. The pilot says he expects a three-hour wait because of the storm moving inland. Ender sits back, taking the time to review the contracts for his meetings in Istanbul.

Concentrating very hard on the terms of the contract, Ender doesn't hear the pilot approach his seat.

"Mr. Dogan, I assume your phone is off because Joseph just called me. There's an emergency, and you need to call him now."

Ender nods, turns on his phone and calls Joseph. "Joseph, what's going on?"

"Ender, there was a carjacking. Valerie is at Mercy Hospital. She's shaken up but will be okay. They killed Burak."

"Why was Valerie taken to Mercy?"

"It was the closest one to their location. I'm almost at the airport to pick you up."

"Great. I'll meet you on the tarmac," Ender replies as anger seeps into his pores. He tells the pilot he'll return soon so they can get to Istanbul before tomorrow. Ender then leaves the plane to wait for Joseph.

Ender walks into the hospital in a rush, followed by Joseph. They gave him Valerie's room number, and quickly Ender bursts into her room. Valerie is awake and surrounded by doctors and nurses.

"Valerie, what in the hell were you doing in that part of Miami?" Ender yells at her, full of anger. "I told you never to go to that part of town. But no, you had to go. Now, I've lost a car and an excellent security officer. I can't trust you to do the simplest things I ask and follow my instructions. I'm going to Istanbul. I'll deal with you when I get back." Ender stomps out of the room. "Take me back to the airport, Joseph."

Joseph tosses Ender the keys. "Drive yourself back," he tells Ender.

Ender catches the keys. "Fine, I'll deal with you too when I return."

Ender returns to the plane. Unfortunately, he is so angry at Valerie and Joseph that he can't concentrate on work. Fortunately, the plane takes off thirty minutes later.

Chapter 41

Valerie

Valerie cries as soon as Ender leaves. Joseph comes in and comforts her.

"That's it, Joseph. I'm leaving and will be gone by the time he returns."

"I'm going with you," Joseph says, taking her hand.

"No, Joseph. You can't," Valerie says, wiping her tears.

"I can and I will. Valerie, I overheard the doctor say you're having twins. You are going to need help. I'm tired of working for Ender. He's not the same man I went to work for years ago. Let's get you out of here and to the apartment."

Valerie checks out of the hospital while Joseph arranges for a taxi to take them back to the apartment. Once there, Joseph helps her to her bedroom.

"Valerie, you must pack your personal items and be prepared to leave quickly. Ender is a loose cannon right now. Take nothing with you except what's yours, the clothes on your back, and the burner phone. I'll take care of the security cameras when the time comes. You must arrange a taxi or car share vehicle to pick you up because we can't leave together. I'll send you instructions on where to go. Do you think you can do that?"

"Yes, Joseph. I'll pack now and be ready at any time." Joseph nods and leaves the room.

Valerie showers, changes clothes, and packs the meager belongings she brought with her in her suitcase. She sets it by the door and waits for further instructions from Joseph.

Chapter 42

Ender

Ender's plane lands in Istanbul before dawn. He couldn't sleep on the plane because he was so angry. Even though his car is waiting, Ender takes a few minutes to check his emails and voice messages on the plane. There is a missed phone call from an unknown number. The caller left a voicemail which Ender starts to delete and then changes his mind. The message was from the doctor that treated Valerie. He asks Ender to call him.

Ender checks the time in Miami and sees that he has to wait several hours. He also has six hours before his appointment. Still angry but somewhat calmer now, Ender goes home and takes a nap. When he wakes, he calls the doctor back.

"Mr. Dogan, this is Dr. Patel. I called you about Ms. Richards."

"What about her?" Ender asks sharply.

"She checked out of the hospital yesterday, and I'm concerned about her."

"Why?"

"Well, she's a very petite woman and pregnant with twins."

"You have got to be kidding me! How far along is she?" Ender asks.

"Well, sir, she's three months pregnant."

"Oh, my gosh," Ender says and disconnects the call. Next, he calls Joseph.

"Ender," Joseph answers.

"Joseph, Valerie is pregnant! The doctor just called and told me." Joseph doesn't say anything. "Did you know?"

"Yes, Ender. I know."

"How long have you known, and why didn't you tell me?" Ender shouts.

"I've known for about a month. It wasn't my place to tell you."

"I have a meeting today that I can't miss. So we'll discuss this when I get back tomorrow."

"Always business first, right Ender? We won't discuss it when you get back. I won't be here." Joseph hangs up the phone.

Ender calls Joseph back several times, and the phone always goes to voicemail. He leaves several messages and then sends multiple texts. Joseph still doesn't answer.

"Dammit, dammit, dammit," Ender yells at the top of his lungs. How could Valerie be so stupid? I assumed she was on the pill, but I should have asked. Maybe they're not mine. Maybe Valerie was messing around with her tutor or someone else. She had a lot of free time during the day. Now I have to fix this mess and deal with Joseph quitting.

Ender calls Andrew and has Andrew postpone all meetings except the one this afternoon. Next, he tells Andrew he has to fly back to Miami tonight and make the arrangements.

Chapter 43

Valerie

Valerie answers her door to find Joseph standing there.

"Joseph."

"Valerie, if you're going to leave, you must do it now. Andrew called and Ender will be back tomorrow morning. Ender called me because he knows you're pregnant. The doctor called and told him."

"Oh no. Will your brother help me?"

"Yes, and he'll help me as well. Ender asked if I knew about the pregnancy, and I told him I did. I told him it wasn't my place to tell him, so I'm sure he's really furious now. I told him I quit, so you and I are leaving today."

"Thank you, Joseph. I have everything packed and ready to go. I can leave now."

"It will take me a few hours to pack my belongings. I'll call my brother on the way back to my room and get him to pick you up at this address. Now you call a taxi and go downstairs. I'll stop the security cameras for thirty minutes, so if anyone tries to find out how you left, they won't see anything. I'll catch up with you later."

"Please be careful, Joseph," Valerie says with a kiss on his cheek.

Five minutes later, Valerie is waiting downstairs for her taxi. She has her tote and suitcase only, just as Joseph instructed. When the cab arrives, Valerie gives the driver the address Joseph gave her. Fifteen minutes later, Valerie walks into a shopping mall where Joseph's brother meets her. He leads her to his car and drives her to a hotel in Fort Lauderdale, an hour away. There is a room waiting for her in the name of Cecilia Jacobs.

Five hours later, Joseph texts her he is outside her hotel door. Valerie runs to the door, throws it open, and hugs Joseph.

"Joseph, I was worried about you."

"I'm fine, Valerie. I'm hungry, and I bet you are, too. So let's order room service, and we'll talk."

Once the food is delivered, Valerie and Joseph sit down to eat. "Valerie, I made some decisions for both of us without consulting you. I made these decisions based on what I thought Ender would do. If you are opposed to any of my choices, please tell me."

"Joseph, I trust you, so tell me what's on your mind."

"Ender is furious. I think he will assume the babies aren't his."

"I left him a note telling him they were, but I had the doctor collect blood samples of the babies for DNA testing if Ender wants to know for sure."

"Valerie, that's brilliant and buys us some time if Ender does that. I believe Ender won't do anything for two or three days. By then, I think he will want the DNA test. With his money, he can probably get the results within a week. Remember that Ender will need to find a replacement for me during this, so that will be on his mind too. Once Ender finds out the babies are his, he will have two choices. One will be to hire someone to find you, or he will assume you want money, and he'll wait for you to contact him demanding money."

"But I don't want his money or anything from him," Valerie says.

"I know that, and you know that, but remember, he had a money-hungry ex-wife who did. Ender thinks all women are after his money. I have an inside contact to inform me about what Ender's doing so we can stay ahead of him."

"Joseph, I'm sorry you must give up Andrew and your job for me."

"Honestly, I've been thinking about leaving Ender for some time. Okay, now here's where we discuss the decisions I've made. First, Ender can be vindictive, so we don't want to be found. A person my brother knows has created new identities for both of us. That means new names, socials, passports, educational documents, backgrounds, everything. I have it all in a safe deposit box. I'll get them tomorrow. You and I will be brother and sister, so we have different last names."

Valerie thinks for a few seconds and says, "so that's why this room is under the name Cecilia Jacobs? So that's me now?"

Joseph nods. "Tomorrow, you will need to close your bank account and open a new one at another bank using your new name."

"Joseph, I don't have a lot of money. I can get by for a few months while I look for a job."

"Don't worry about money. I have more than I will ever be able to spend. Ender paid dearly for my services. To continue, your storage building has been emptied, and everything has been loaded onto a rental truck. My brother already has a buyer for my pickup."

"Where are we going?" Valerie asks.

"I have always wanted to work with clay, so I thought we could go to a place where artists of all types live. I bought a place in such an area five years ago."

"Joseph, this sounds exciting. Tell me more."

"The house needs a little work, but it's livable. I checked on it right before you went to work for Ender. The name of the town is Marfa. It is in West Texas, a fairly remote area. It is about twenty-five miles from Alpine and the hospital. There's a university in Alpine if you want to apply for a job teaching."

"Oh wow," Valerie exclaims.

"My plan is for you and me to drive the rental truck to Marfa over the next few days. We could leave tomorrow after you finish with your bank business. You should buy some clothes tomorrow as well. I have mine with me. We can buy a car once we get there."

"You have really thought this whole thing out. I'm impressed, Joseph. I have a request, though."

"Thanks. I did this kind of work in the military. What would you like?"

"Is there any way to set up a secure way to send Ender emails with no one being able to track them? You know. Like scammers use."

"Why do you want that?"

"Well," Valerie sighs, "the babies are Ender's. I know he doesn't want any, but I would like to send him pictures of them periodically so he can see what he helped make."

"Okay, Valerie. I'll get that set up, but keep in mind, you or I will need to Photoshop the pictures, so we don't give away our location."

"I understand. Joseph, I'm getting tired."

"I know. The banks open at 9:00 am. I'll be here for breakfast at 8:00. After we eat, we'll check out, go to my safe deposit box, and then go to your bank. My brother will meet us in the rental truck and take my pickup. Then we can say goodbye to Ender and Miami."

"Okay. Good night, Joseph, and thanks again."

After breakfast the following morning, Valerie and Joseph execute his plans and leave Miami at 11:30. They stop in Tallahassee to buy Valerie clothes and spend the night before heading to their new home and life in Marfa.

Chapter 44

Ender

Before his meeting, Ender sits down with Andrew and his security man. He instructs Andrew to contact Burak's family and make the necessary arrangements for Burak's body to be returned to Turkey. Ender tells Andrew he will pay for all the costs, including funeral expenses. He also tells Andrew to contact Ender's attorney because the family will probably sue the company and Ender. Next, Ender asks the security man if he knows anyone seeking a security job because there are two openings with Ender's firm. The man says he knows two people that might be interested and he will contact them immediately.

Ender is very distracted during his business meeting. Fortunately, the meeting is with a longtime acquaintance, and he asks Ender what's wrong. Ender replies one of his security detail was killed in a carjacking, and his head security man quit. The business acquaintance tells Ender he will talk to his security people about prospects for Ender. The two men agree to meet again in two weeks to discuss the contract.

Because Ender is flying back to Miami sooner than planned, Andrew flies with him. The entire flight is quiet. Ender tries to sleep but cannot. Since Joseph won't respond to Ender's calls or texts, Ender decides to check Joseph's personnel file when he gets home for an emergency contact. Even though Joseph quit, he has been Ender's friend for a long time. Perhaps, he will help Ender find two new security people.

It surprises Ender how quiet the apartment is when he returns home. He goes to his bedroom; pleased Valerie isn't there. Valerie. I haven't thought about her or what to do with her at all. I've been so focused on security that I forgot. An inner voice says you didn't forget at all. You just didn't want to think about it. He throws his jacket and tie on the bed and heads to his office.

Joseph's personnel file is at the very back of Ender's file cabinet, so it takes Ender several minutes to find it. Joseph has listed a brother as his emergency contact. Even though it is late, Ender dials the number.

"Hello," a sleepy voice answers.

"Are you Joseph Rizzo's brother?"

"It depends on who wants to know."

Ender shakes his head and takes a deep breath before answering. "This is Ender Dogan. Joseph worked for me."

"Okay, what do you want?"

"I need to talk to Joseph. Do you have a number where I can reach him?"

"Look, fellow. I haven't heard from Joseph in years. Don't call hear again." The phone disconnects.

Well, that was a dead end, Ender thinks, frustrated. My whole life is going up in flames before my eyes, and I can't do anything about it. I guess I better deal with Valerie now. He walks to her bedroom door and knocks. There's no answer. Ender enters the dark bedroom. It has an icy feeling to it, but it smells of jasmine and Valerie. Ender turns on the light, expecting to find Valerie in bed, but the bed is empty and hasn't been slept in. In the middle of the bed lies an envelope with his name and the allergy necklace he had specially made for Valerie. Ender rips open the envelope and reads:

Ender,

Many times it is easier to write the words than say them. Since you were a raving lunatic in the hospital, you didn't give me a chance to talk. You didn't even ask how I was, which really hurt, but it wasn't a surprise to me knowing you are a busy, important man.

Yes, I was in a bad part of Miami, but I went to a clinic there to end the pregnancy, which I knew you would have wanted. You said you didn't want kids several times and hated them. But once I got to the clinic, I realized this is my life, not yours. I was going to lose everything related to you, anyway, so I chose to keep the babies. They will always be a reminder of my special time with you. I am very sorry Burak lost his life saving mine, and I will always be grateful to him for that.

You probably think I slept with another man since you told me you couldn't see yourself committed to one woman. I didn't, and to prove it; I asked the doctor to take blood samples of the babies so you could run DNA tests if you wish. All you have to do is call the doctor, provide your sample, and the doctor will take care of the rest.

You said you didn't know what love was, so you wouldn't know how to give or receive it. That is so true of you. You see, I fell in love with you and tried to show it in every way, especially when I gave myself to you. But you just assumed I was another horny woman who could resist a handsome man like yourself. Maybe someday you will find out what love is. I hope you do, but it won't be with me.

So now you probably think I left because of the babies or because I love you. The answer is no. The truthful answer lies in the conditions I gave you when I accepted the job you offered. You don't remember? I'm not surprised. I will not tell you. If you are the least bit interested, read your notes in my personnel file. The answer will be there.

So I'm off to raise our babies. I hope when they are old enough, I will have thought of a nice way to explain why their father didn't want them.

Love now and forever,

Valerie

Ender reads the letter twice more, letting the words sink in. Finally, he picks up the necklace, holds it to his heart, and remembers when he gave it to Valerie. A simple, relatively inexpensive gift that made her eyes light up, and her smile was breathtaking. Ender turns the light off and inhales the scent of jasmine deeply before closing the door. He is exhausted, having no sleep in forty-eight hours, so he showers and climbs into bed after laying the letter and necklace on his bedside table.

Lying on his back, Ender turns over toward Valerie's pillow. He needs to hold and kiss her to fall asleep, but she's not there. He grabs her pillow, which still smells of her, and holds it to his chest. His mind won't stop. He turns on the lamp and rereads the letter. Valerie is gone and pregnant with twins. She fell in love with him and tried to show him, but he was so wrapped up in himself that he didn't see it.

He rereads the last paragraph. I have to know why Valerie said she left, but I can't do that now. Her file is at the office. Then Ender does something he never does. After climbing out of bed, he pours a large glass of Scotch in the kitchen. He drinks it and then another one. Finally, he stumbles to bed and eventually falls asleep, clutching Valerie's pillow.

The following morning, Ender is at the office early. First, he tells his secretary to cancel all his daily meetings. Next, he calls the doctor and schedules an appointment for 9:00 am to give a DNA sample. Then, Ender pulls Valerie's personnel file out of his credenza and scans his interview notes. It takes a few minutes, but finally, Ender finds what he is looking for. Not only did he write her stipulations down, but Ender also put them in quotation marks to emphasize their importance.

He reads them aloud. Valerie said, "I need time to get things in order. I also need to make arrangements for my car and apartment. Second, never chastise me in the presence of others. If you have an issue with me, please talk to me in private. Third, never talk down to me. I am a human being and merit respect from you and others. If you are ever condescending to me, I won't stay with you."

Ender put his hands on each side of his head and rereads the second and third conditions. "Damn. I did exactly what she asked me not to do. At the hospital, I did it in front of doctors, nurses, and anyone else listening. I have never done that to any employee. Yet, I did it to her. Valerie said she wouldn't stay if I ever did, and she left me just like she said she would. It's all my fault she left. I have to do something."

When Ender leaves the hospital, he goes straight home. He has the security men pull all the surveillance tapes from the last week. As they do, they remind him he requested all the cameras be turned off in the apartment when Valerie moved in. Unfortunately, the security men are forced to listen to a tirade of foul language while pulling footage from outside the building. The cameras show Valerie leaving with Burak the day she went to the clinic. Then they show her returning home with Joseph in a taxi later that day. That's the last Valerie is seen. There's no way to know when she left.

Knowing Valerie has no family, Ender's next move is to report Valerie as a missing person to the police. He decides to wait on the DNA test results, which the doctor said would take a week. Besides, Valerie isn't rich, so Ender expects her to call or email and demand money for her and the babies. All the women he has ever met are only after money and the material things it can buy.

Ender's phone rings, and his heart beats faster. It is Valerie, he silently hopes, but it is Andrew.

"Mr. Dogan, I sent Ms. Richards' final salary payment to her bank, but it was returned. They said the account was closed. What can I do?"

"Andrew, I don't know. Did they tell you when the account was closed?"

"No, sir. They said they couldn't release that information."

"Okay, then just hold on to the funds for now. Valerie will contact us when she needs the money."

Ender does the only thing he knows to do at this point. He sets up a video chat with his therapist, who is available in thirty minutes. Ender tries to gather his thoughts before the meeting, but his mind is racing like a hamster on a wheel.

"Ender, what can I do for you?" the therapist asks when the video chat begins. Ender goes through all the events of the past few days. He reads Valerie's letter to him and tells him why she left.

"So, Ender, do you think the babies are yours?"

"Yes, I believe they are. But, knowing Valerie, I'm not surprised she decided against terminating the pregnancy. She will make an exceptional mother," Ender states.

"How do you feel about the babies?" the therapist asks.

"I don't want kids. Never did and still don't."

"Do you really think she will demand money?" Ender is quiet for a few seconds. "Ender, I asked you a question."

"No, I don't think she will." The therapist detects a note of sadness in Ender's voice. "If the babies are mine, I would be happy to give her money to ensure all three are provided for, but she won't ask."

"I think you're right. Now, how do you feel about all this?"

"Honestly, doctor, I'm so confused. I can't eat. I can't sleep. It's like I'm walking around in one of those carnival tents where mirrors surround you, and you can't find your way out."

The therapist contemplates Ender's state of mind and then says, "I can send you some pills to help you sleep, but there's more to it, isn't there, Ender? Did you ever tell Valerie how you felt?"

"No, I couldn't because I didn't understand it myself. I still don't. I feel guilty about Valerie leaving, and I miss her so much. I miss everything about her. I won't let the housekeeper wash the bedding because it smells like Valerie. Sometimes, I feel like I'm having a heart attack because my heart aches so bad," Ender says.

"Ender, do you feel guilty because Valerie fell in love with you?"

Ender ponders the question before answering. "Yes, not because she did, but because I don't deserve her love. Okay, now you've asked me all these questions, and I answered them. Now what? I don't feel any better."

"Ender, I believe you are in love with Valerie. You just won't admit it. Your heart aches because it is broken, and you miss her. I believe your guilt is from not telling her you love her. As far as deserving her love, I think you do because you've changed. You're a different man because of Valerie. Like I said, I'll drop you something to help you sleep. You might contact one of your whores to help get your mind off Valerie."

"That's not an option," Ender says. "I don't want to be with any woman but Valerie." Ender pauses. "Dammit, I just admitted I want to be committed to one woman, didn't I?"

The therapist laughs. "Yes, Ender, you did. Now, go find Valerie, so you both can heal your broken hearts."

After the video chat ends, Ender goes to the police station and files a missing person report. The police officer he talks to tells Ender they are overrun with missing people. He suggests Ender hire a private investigator. The police will work with the investigator. On the way home, Ender sends a message to Andrew to find the best one in the US.

Chapter 45

Valerie

It took four days to drive to Marfa because Joseph didn't want Valerie to get too tired. Once they arrived at Joseph's house, the pair rested, and then Joseph found two men to help him unload the rental truck. Next, Joseph purchased an older model pickup and turned the rental truck in. Then, the pair went in search of a doctor for Valerie. Finally, they had to go to Alpine to find an obstetrician and were able to get an appointment for the next day.

After they return home, Joseph gets a message from Andrew telling Joseph that Ender is confused, unable to sleep and filed a missing person report on Valerie with the police. Ender is currently having Andrew search for a private investigator. He also says that Ender is having the DNA test done.

When Joseph reads the message to Valerie, she shakes her head. "I'm not surprised Ender's going through with the test. I don't think he ever fully trusted me."

"Oh, he trusted you, alright. It is himself he never trusted. He's very insecure. I'm glad he's doing it. I bet he's waiting for you to contact him, asking him for money."

"Well, he'll have a long wait. After my doctor's appointment tomorrow, I'll go to the university and ask about jobs."

"Valerie, you don't have to do that. I told you I have plenty of money."

"I know, but I can't expect you to pay for my keep and the babies," Valerie says. "Maybe if I can get a job, I can get medical insurance."

"Okay, do whatever you want, but remember, you don't have to. While you're gone, I'll research how to get started on pottery and what supplies I'll need."

"Joseph, what a great idea. I think you'll be fantastic at it."

The following day, Valerie's appointment goes well. The doctor orders several tests and prescribes prenatal vitamins for Valerie. After the tests, Valerie goes to the university. It surprises her to learn they are searching for a faculty member to teach undergraduate business courses. There would be four classes per week, and the classes are online so that Valerie could work from home. She applies for the job using her fake vita information and fake credentials.

It is late in the day when she returns home to find Joseph has dinner ready. Valerie tells him about the appointment, tests, and job she applied for. Joseph talks about what he discovered about pottery, and there is a supply store in Alpine. The pair makes plans to visit the store the following day and pick up Valerie's vitamins.

Chapter 46

Ender

Ender receives the DNA test results one week after submitting his sample. He is definitely the father of the twins. It surprises him he feels a little excited and emotional about being a father. Ender wonders how Valerie is and if she's showing yet. He reads articles on the internet about pregnancy, the birth of twins, and the mother's health.

He's found and hired a private investigator to search for Valerie. With the police's help, the investigator views the bank's camera footage and finds out when Valerie closed her account. The street cameras show Valerie arriving in a taxi, but when she leaves the bank, she walks around a corner and is never seen again.

The investigator also discovers that Valerie's storage unit was emptied two days before she closed her bank account. Therefore, the investigator believes either Valerie had planned to disappear in advance or had help. The investigator also finds no leads on Joseph, who also closed his bank accounts and sold his pickup. Ender tells the investigator he believes Joseph is helping Valerie because they disappeared around the same time. With Joseph's military background, no one may ever find him or Valerie.

Ender remembers how he ran into Valerie two years after Joseph bumped into her in Istanbul. It was fate. Perhaps someday fate will bring him and Valerie together again. "I can only hope," Ender says aloud.

Chapter 47

Valerie

The next six months go by quickly for Valerie. She gets a teaching job at the university with medical benefits and can now pay some of her own way. She works from home while she grows larger with her two babies. Even though Joseph said nothing, it makes Valerie feel better.

The twins are born by cesarian section at eight and half months because of Valerie's petite size and her blood pressure. The boy and girl are healthy, but the pregnancy leaves Valerie with a weakened heart and on medication. As a result, she will not be able to have any more children. When the doctor clears her to return to work, Joseph hires a lady to help Valerie with the babies while she recovers.

"Joseph, I would like to send Ender pictures of the babies," Valerie says.

"Okay, let me contact my guy and get everything set up."

Several days later, Valerie dresses the babies in cute outfits, and Joseph takes many pictures. Together they decide which pictures to send to Ender and Photoshop backgrounds into the images so their location cannot be identified. Finally, Valerie sends the four photos of the twins together and two of each individually.

Chapter 48

Ender

"**M**r. Dogan, you know I check your emails as they come in, but I only check the junk emails weekly. I found an email that came in three days ago that I think you better look at," Andrew says, walking into Ender's office. "I forwarded it to you."

"Is it important enough for me to look at now?" Ender asks.

"It is, in my opinion, and I suggest you look at it on your laptop instead of your phone." Ender nods and opens his email account as Andrew leaves.

He searches the emails by date and finds those from three days ago. There is one email that catches his eye immediately. The subject line reads "For You!" There is no message in the email, only pictures that must be downloaded. Ender clicks on the link, and the images of his babies appear.

The twins are a boy and a girl. The boy favors Valerie, with dark brown hair and eyes. The girl favors Ender with blond hair and hazel eyes. Both are dressed in cute clothing. Four pictures show the twins together. Then there are two pictures of each one individually. Ender studies each photo for a very long time. In one picture of the boy, he is crying, and his face is red. However, it is the boy's eyes that grab Ender's attention. The amber flecks of Valerie are in the boy's eyes.

Ender locks his office door and sits back down at his desk. He lies his head down on his crossed arms and cries, which he has never done before. Valerie was thoughtful enough to send him pictures of their beautiful babies. Ender's arms ache to hold Valerie and tell her how beautiful the babies are. He cries because he wasn't there with her when they were born. After a while, Ender dries his eyes, saves the photos to his laptop, and then sends copies to an online company to make them into 8x10 photos.

Finally, Ender forwards the email to his private investigator. He tells the investigator to find out where the email originated and determine the photos' location. Plus, Ender wants him to search for twins born in the US in the last sixty days, especially those born to women named Valerie. Ender knows Valerie probably took steps to prevent him from finding her, but he has to try.

Chapter 49

Valerie

Over the next two years, Valerie sends Ender pictures of the twins every three months so he can see them grow and change. In addition, she continues her teaching job from home. Joseph's pottery is beautiful, and he's selling it online, but with Valerie's marketing skills, his pottery is being displayed in a gallery in Dallas for one month. The gallery requests Joseph attend the grand opening, and he hates to leave Valerie, but she insists.

"No one should recognize you with your beard and mustache," Valerie insists a week before he has to leave.

"I know, but I'm still worried," Joseph replies. Together they make plans in case they or their location is discovered. Joseph tells Valerie he will text her the word "*END*" if he senses a problem. She is to have a bag packed for her and the babies in the car at all times so she can leave quickly. Since Joseph's contact has arranged several identities for them, Valerie will pick one and leave Texas immediately. She is to let Joseph's brother know her location so Joseph can find her.

Valerie and the twins take Joseph to the Midland/Odessa airport a week later for his trip to Dallas. Although he is very apprehensive about leaving, Valerie is excited because Joseph is finally gaining recognition for his beautiful work. He kisses her on the cheek before getting out of the car and tells her he will see her in a week. As Joseph tells the twins goodbye, tears come to his eyes. He hates to leave, knowing he may not see them again.

One week later, Valerie picks up an excited Joseph at the airport. The exhibit is a success. Several people are interested in his work for their businesses, including two from hotels. In addition, most of the pottery has been sold, so he doesn't have to worry about having it shipped back. Before heading home, Joseph takes Valerie and the twins out for a celebratory dinner.

Chapter 50

Ender

"**C**ome on, Ender. Show a little more enthusiasm," the interior decorator says. "I know you'll love this man's work as much as I do.

Ender steps off the plane. "I'll tell you what I know. I let you drag me to a place in the middle of nowhere. This place is so small I had to charter a smaller jet just to get here."

"Ender, it's your fault you're here. You wanted to have the final say in the décor of the hotel lobby. Besides, you should be excited. The hotel will be finished in a couple of months. You've sold all the condos and are making the new owners pay for renovations. That will save you a ton of money. Let's get the rental car."

"Do they even have rental cars here?" Ender looks around at the small airport.

The decorator rolls her eyes. "Well, I didn't rent a horse and buggy if that's what you are insinuating. Enjoy the fresh air. You've become a hermit the last three years." The pair walk toward the small terminal. "You hardly visited the construction site and rarely left the apartment. You stopped attending social functions and haven't returned to Turkey."

"Where do you get all your information?" Ender asks sharply.

"From Andrew, of course." The decorator signs the paperwork for the rental car and grabs the keys. "I don't know what's going on with you, but Andrew has had a hard three years himself."

"Why? He said nothing."

"Would you have noticed if he had?" Ender shrugs his shoulders in answer. "Andrew lost the love of his life when Joseph left."

"What?" Ender yells.

"Really? You didn't know they were together?" Ender looks at the decorator in astonishment and shakes his head. "Boy, you really do live under a rock. Do you want to drive, or shall I?"

"You drive so that way you'll have to focus on the directions and not on my life," Ender replies harshly, climbing into the car.

"We are fortunate this guy agreed to let us visit his shop and gallery. He's a very private person. I wouldn't have known about him at all if I hadn't visited the gallery in Dallas."

The drive is short but gives Ender time to think. Andrew and Joseph were a couple. Here I thought about Valerie and Joseph marrying and having more babies. Joseph isn't interested in women. Thank goodness for that.

Ender observes that the building is old and looks rundown, as does the house sitting next to it. However, a newer car and a pickup are parked between the two buildings. "Are you sure this is the right place?" he asks.

The decorator replies, "this is the address. These artists are very temperamental, so I bet the inside looks much better. Let's go."

As they walk toward the building, Ender hears children's laughter coming from the direction of the house. A little bell rings, signaling Ender and the decorator's entrance to the building. While they wait, Ender looks around at a state-of-the-art workroom.

A man approaches them from a back room and welcomes them. The man is large and muscular, with jet-black hair pulled back into a ponytail, a thick black beard, and a mustache. As he walks toward them, he quickly types something into his phone and places it in his pocket. He introduces himself as Jason Whitlow and shakes the decorator's hand.

As Ender offers his hand, he looks directly into Joseph's eyes. Before Ender can say anything, the sound of a car engine starting causes him to look out the window. As the car passes by, Ender sees Valerie behind the wheel. "Give me the keys," he shouts to the decorator, who tosses them at him. Ender runs from the building as the car turns onto the highway.

With his heart racing, Ender jumps into the rental car and speeds after Valerie. She is a skillful driver and drives faster and faster along the quiet country road. Fortunately, there are no other cars on the road. Ender is excited about finding Valerie but tries to keep his thoughts on his driving as he follows her. Suddenly, he hears what sounds like an explosion and sees Valerie's car wobbling and slowing down. Finally, the car stops, so Ender pulls in front of Valerie to block her in. He jumps out of the car and races toward her. He notices the front tire blew out, which caused Valerie to have to stop. Giddy with happiness, Ender knocks on the window. But his joy is short-lived when he sees the terror in Valerie's eyes.

"Ender," Valerie says. Then she grabs her chest and slumps over the steering wheel. Ender tries to open the door, but it's locked. He hears the twins in the back seat yelling "papa" and crying. Ender tries all the doors on the car and the latch on the trunk, but all are locked. He looks around for a large rock, hoping to find one to break the window. Just then, Joseph and the decorator pull in behind Valerie's car.

"Something's wrong with Valerie. All the doors are locked, and I can't get in," Ender yells.

"I've got a key," Joseph yells back. "Ender, call 911 now!" Ender dials 911 and watches as Joseph unlocks the door and kneels beside Valerie. Joseph checks her pulse and leans Valerie back in the seat. "It's her heart," he tells Ender quietly. The twins are still crying, so Joseph opens the car's back door and tries to soothe them. Ender kneels beside Valerie and holds her hand, terrified he may have lost her again. Finally, the ambulance arrives and loads Valerie inside.

"Ender, take my truck and follow the ambulance. I'll change the tire and then take the car and the kids to a friend's house. Then I'll be there. They won't give you any information about her, so just be patient. Valerie will be fine."

Ender nods. He tells the decorator to go to the plane as soon as she can get there. She should fly back to Miami and not say a word to anyone about this. "Business can wait a week or two." She replies she understands and leaves.

After arriving at the hospital, all Ender can do is wait for Joseph. Then, finally, after what seems like a lifetime, Joseph walks into the waiting room and sits down.

"Ender, it's her heart. It is weak. It all started during the later part of the pregnancy. Valerie had to have the twins by C-section because of her size and blood pressure. The doctors are trying to control it with medication."

"Will she be okay?" Ender asks, tears rolling down his cheeks.

Before Joseph can answer, Valerie's doctor walks in. He shakes hands with Joseph, who then introduces Ender as the twin's father.

"Valerie has a heart valve that's leaking. I think it's been a tiny leak for a long time, probably contributing to her weakened heart or causing it. The leak has increased to the point now where she needs surgery immediately. Unfortunately, I can't do the surgery here. She will need to be transferred to Midland Memorial."

"How fast can you get her there?" Ender asks.

"I have already requested a medical helicopter, so she should be on her way within an hour. I have a good friend there who will wait for her. Dr. Ventura is an excellent cardiologist and surgeon. She is planning to do the surgery once Valerie arrives."

"What are her chances?" Ender asks.

"This type of surgery is fairly common. Once Dr. Ventura opens Valerie up, she will determine if the valve can be repaired or needs to be replaced. Valerie should fully recover and be in cardiac rehab for a short period."

"Joseph, Valerie will be limited to the weight she can lift, so I suggest you get help with the twins and maybe a short time nurse for Valerie. I don't expect her hospital stay to be longer than two or three days. If you have no other questions, I suggest you leave now to complete all the paperwork for Valerie's check-in before she arrives." Joseph and Ender shake the doctor's hand as he leaves.

"Well, Ender? What's it going to be? Should I take you to the airport, or are you going with me?" Joseph asks.

"I'm going with you. There's no way I'm letting Valerie out of my sight again."

"Fine. Let's go. We can talk on the drive to the hospital."

Chapter 51

Valerie

Valerie opens her eyes slightly to see the room is mostly dark except for a light behind her. She inhales the cool air and hears a constant beeping sound. Valerie turns her head and looks at the source of the beeping. Well, I guess I'm in the hospital; she thinks. Drowsily, she turns her head to her right and sees a man slumped over the side of her bed, asleep. My dear friend Joseph is always with me, no matter what. Valerie lifts her hand and places it on the man's head softly. The man's hair is shorter than Joseph's and is almost blond. Oh, my gosh! It's Ender. Valerie lays her hand back down, closes her eyes, and tries to remember what happened. The chain of events plays in her mind like a video.

Valerie is playing with the kids in the backyard. They are building a castle out of wooden blocks. Her phone rings with a message from Joseph that says "*END*," his code for leave immediately. "Dammit," Valerie says aloud, knowing Ender found them. She grabs the twins and buckles them into their car seats quickly. Next, Valerie runs into the house and grabs her purse and car keys. Then she gets into the car and drives off.

It is only seconds before a car is behind her. No matter how fast she drives, the car matches her speed. Valerie slows down slightly and lets the car catch up so she can look at the driver in her rearview mirror. "Dammit, it's Ender." Being at the age to repeat things they've heard, the twins yell "dammit" and laugh. Valerie is too engrossed in driving to correct the twins, so she lets them continue chanting and giggling. Valerie increases her speed and gives silent thanks that no one else is on the road.

Then the car makes a loud pop and starts wobbling. "Dammit," Valerie says aloud again, making the twins laugh, and they repeat the word repeatedly. Valerie knows a tire has blown and struggles to control the car and slow down. Finally, she brings it to a stop and puts it into parking gear. Valerie watches as Ender jumps from his vehicle and races toward her. Her chest begins hurting. The twins see Ender and start yelling "Papa" and crying. Ender knocks on her window and calls her name. Valerie grips her chest, and then everything goes black.

When Valerie wakes up a couple of hours later, Ender sits beside her bed, holding her hand. "Ender, what are you doing here?" she asks.

"Waiting for you to wake up and ask me to kiss you," he replies with a grin.

Valerie rolls her eyes. "Always teasing me, aren't you?"

"Well, if I have to be serious, the truth is I'm waiting for the love of my life and the mother of our babies to wake up. I need to tell her I'm a complete idiot and will never let her go again."

She studies Ender for several minutes. His looks have changed somewhat. He is paler, and his eyes look tired but have softened. There are tiny wrinkles at the corners of them. His hair is longer and curls at the back of his neck against his shirt collar. His shoulders are slightly hunched over and don't appear as broad as they once were. He's thinner, making his shirt hang loosely across his chest.

"You look different," Valerie says.

"I guess spending the last three years searching for you has done that to me."

"Did you really search for me?"

"Every moment of every day since the day I found your letter. Valerie, I'm so sorry I hurt you. I want to spend the rest of my life making it up to you if you'll let me," Ender says as tears form in his eyes and roll down his cheeks.

"We can talk about this later," Valerie says, wiping his tears with a corner from the sheet covering her body. "Tell me what happened."

Ender describes her blacking out and Joseph driving up. Joseph took the twins to a friend's house while Ender followed the ambulance. He tells her about the surgery and that she is in a hospital in Midland. Ender says the surgery replaced a heat valve, and Valerie should be better than before and off medication after rehab. He also tells her she can go home in two days.

Someone knocks on the door, and Joseph appears with a huge grin, carrying an enormous bouquet. He kisses her cheek and tells her the twins are fine and demanding to see their mom.

"I bet they were happy to see you when you got to the car," Ender says. "They kept calling papa."

Valerie and Joseph look at each other. "Ender, they were calling for you," Joseph says softly.

Ender looks back and forth between Joseph and Valerie. "I don't understand," he says.

"Papa is their name for you," Valerie says. "Joseph is Uncle Joe."

"Are you telling me the twins know who I am?" Ender asks in shock.

"Do you really think I would raise our children without knowing their father? I always talked about you and showed them pictures of you."

"That's true," Joseph says. "I got so sick of hearing about you and how perfect you were. Valerie made you sound like a much better person than you are."

"Then where did you tell them I was since I wasn't there?"

Valerie grins. "I told them you were a busy, important man who worked in another country. I told them you would come for them and take them to your home one day."

"And what about their mother? Would I take her home, too?" Ender asks.

"I told them you would take only them," Valerie whispers.

Ender reaches up and caresses her cheek. "I thought it was a package deal. You and the twins. At least, that's what I hope for."

Valerie pulls her head away. "Ender, I would like some time alone with Joseph now."

"Ender, here are the keys to my truck. I have rooms rented at a hotel two blocks away. Why don't you go, clean up, and get some sleep? Andrew is there waiting for you with clean clothes. I'll stay with Valerie," Joseph tells him. "The jet is also at the airport if you want to return to Miami."

"I'm not leaving except to go to the hotel." Ender leans over and whispers, "I love you," in Valerie's ear. Then he turns and leaves the room.

"Joseph, what do we do now?" Valerie asks once Ender is gone.

"It's your call, Valerie. Ender appears to have changed. I talked to Andrew at length. He said Ender never told him what was wrong, but Ender shut down. He rarely left the apartment as if waiting for you to return. Ender was very lax in his business dealings, especially the hotel, which opens in a couple of months. Basically, Andrew said he would describe Ender as severely depressed and in mourning. Ender has been on sleeping pills and antidepressants ever since you left."

"I don't know what to do, Joseph. My heart tells me one thing, and my brain another. Ender seems to have changed a little. Maybe we can just see how things go for a couple of weeks. Ender won't stay here forever. He's got things he needs to deal with whether he wants to. On another note, I know you were thrilled to see Andrew."

"Ender hasn't left your side since you came out of surgery. As far as Andrew goes, I was thrilled and still am. We talked nonstop for twelve hours after he arrived and talked about our future. He wants to stay with Ender until Ender gets back on his feet. Then he wants to quit, and we can start a life together."

"Oh, Joseph, that's wonderful. I'm so happy for you. You both have waited a long time to be together."

"Yes, we have, but I'm not abandoning you. I will always take care of you first. We have plenty of fake IDs and plans if we need to leave quickly and disappear."

"I know. Now, tell me how my babies are."

Chapter 52

Ender

Ender is a mixture of motions as he drives to the hotel. After a good hot shower, he orders room service and has the first hot meal since the day he and the decorator left for Marfa. After he's finished, Ender lies on the bed, but sleep doesn't come immediately. Instead, Ender's mind replays Valerie, telling him the twins were calling out for him, their papa. They know who he is because their wonderful mother told them about him and showed them pictures.

But what keeps Ender awake is that Valerie told them one day Ender will come for them, not her, and take them home. I have to prove that I want us to be a family and love Valerie with all my heart. I wonder if she still loves me after all this time. Finally, Ender falls asleep without his sleeping pills.

"Ender. Ender," the voice says as someone shakes him. Ender turns toward the voice and opens his eyes to find Andrew standing over him.

"How long have I been asleep?"

"Twelve hours. I finally decided I needed to check to see if you were still alive," Andrew answers.

"Oh, no. I've got to get to the hospital. Valerie will think I left," Ender jumps out of bed and starts searching for clothes.

"Ender, wait. I've talked to Joseph. He's still with Valerie, and she's been sleeping off and on herself. So you don't have to rush to get there. I've ordered food. It will be here in about twenty minutes, so why don't you shower and dress? We have things to discuss first, and then you can go to the hospital."

"Okay, Andrew, and yes, we need to talk about many things."

"How do you feel?" Andrew asks when a dressed Ender walks into the suite's living area.

"Great. Thanks for bringing me some clothes." Andrew nods and points to the food he has laid on the small dining table. Ender sits down. "Now, Andrew, we need to talk seriously about you and Joseph. Why didn't you tell me you were a couple?"

"You never cared to know about my personal life or my life," Andrew answers honestly. "I worked for you. We weren't friends or anything. As far as Joseph goes, I don't believe you cared about him either, at least not the way a genuine friend would."

Ender hangs his head. "You're right, Andrew. I only cared about myself. I want to do better. I want to be a better person, and I think I can, with Valerie's help."

"What are you working to do about Valerie and the twins?"

Ender looks at Andrew in surprise. "What do you know about Valerie and the twins?"

"I know just about everything, duh. Remember Joseph and I are friends?"

"Did you know where they were all this time?" Ender asks angrily.

"No, of course not. Joseph wouldn't jeopardize their safety by telling me that. I knew they were together when the twins were born. I'm your assistant, remember? All your phone calls, emails, and texts are accessible to me. What I didn't know was how you felt about Valerie. You didn't either for a very long time."

"Yeah, you're right about that, but I know now. Somehow I have to make her understand how I feel, so she'll return to me. I just hope she still loves me."

"I don't think you have to worry, boss. I doubt she would have sent those pictures of the twins to a man she hated. You've got a lot of time to make up for. What's your plan?"

"Well, for starters, gather up your things. You're coming to the hospital with me."

Valerie is asleep when Ender and Andrew arrive, so Ender calls Joseph out into the hallway. First, Ender apologizes for being away for so long. Joseph laughs and replies he knows Ender is exhausted.

Ender asks Joseph about plans for Valerie when she returns home. Joseph has hired a nanny for the twins and a nurse for Valerie. He plans to ask about medical equipment when the doctor visits Valerie later in the day. Valerie will need cardiac rehab for about a month, so she must go to Alpine three times a week.

Ender says he isn't leaving. Ender instructs Andrew to find a hotel in Marfa where he and Andrew can stay for at least a month. Then he tells Andrew to contact the decorator and have her return in two weeks to meet with Joseph about the pottery. Ender insists on paying for all of Valerie's care, so Joseph tells Ender about Valerie's teaching position and her insurance. Ender states he will pay for everything the insurance doesn't cover.

A short time later, the doctor examines Valerie and is pleased. They will release her from the hospital tomorrow morning. He tells Joseph no medical equipment is required but says he will sedate her for the long drive home. After that, Valerie will not have to return to the hospital, so her doctor in Alpine can oversee her recovery.

Ender desperately wants to be the one to take Valerie home, but Joseph has taken excellent care of her after she left. Ender suggests Joseph go to the hotel and rest so he can drive Valerie home tomorrow. Andrew and Joseph will drive to Marfa after Joseph returns. Ender sees tears well up in Joseph's eyes and knows that the simple gesture he made means a great deal to Joseph.

Chapter 53

Valerie

Valerie opens her eyes as Ender walks into her room with a big grin. "Hey, I hear you get to go home tomorrow," he says.

"Yes, so you can go home now. I'll be fine."

"I don't want to go home; when I do, I want you and the twins to go with me."

Valerie looks directly into his eyes. "I wish I could believe you, Ender. I really do."

"Look, I know I've made many mistakes, and it has taken me a while to realize that. I just need to know if you still love me and will give me a chance to make things up to you," Ender says as he sits beside the bed and takes her hand in his.

Tears fill Valerie's eyes and start running down her cheeks. "I have never stopped loving you," she whispers.

Ender brushes her tears away with his thumb. "Thank you for that. I love you very much," he says, kissing her hand.

"When, Ender? When did you start loving me, and when did you realize it?"

"I have given it a lot of thought. I think I fell in love with you when I kissed your cupid bow lips while you were asleep from the pain medication."

"That was years ago."

"I know. My heart fell in love with you then, but it took my brain a long time to understand it. After you left, I realized that the hurt and pain I felt could only be because my heart was broken. I was no longer a whole person because the best part of me was gone."

"Ender, why didn't you tell me how you felt?"

"I couldn't tell you about something I didn't know and understand. My therapist helped me discover my feelings were love. I knew how you were with me was special somehow, but I didn't know how special until you were gone. I had never made love to a woman before you. I never wanted to, but with you, everything was different. Everything was new and glorious and exciting and so very intimate. Valerie, I haven't touched a woman since you. I have been waiting for you and only you. You are the woman I want to be with for the rest of my life. I will do anything you ask to prove it to you."

"I just don't know, Ender. I guess we can take it one day at a time."

"Okay. I can live with that. Now, I need to tell you that Andrew and I will stay in Marfa for as long as it takes. I may have to periodically leave for a day or two to get the hotel's grand opening done, but I will return to you. I want to get to know the twins and start being a father to them. I don't know how, but I hope you will teach me."

"You'll be a good father, Ender. There's nothing to teach. You just love them, listen to them, and hope for the best. That's what I did. Here comes the nurse. I need to get up and walk. Will you walk with me?"

The way down the hallway begins in an uncomfortable silence. Then Ender says, "Valerie, what are our children's names?"

She looks at him and smiles. "Your son's name is Sean Ender, and your daughter's name is Sophie Ecrin."

"You gave them American and Turkish names?"

"Of course. That is the blood that courses through their bodies."

"And you gave the boy my name?" Ender asks, astonished.

"I don't know why you're surprised. He's your son, although your daughter takes after you more than he does," Valerie laughs. "You're going to have your hands full with her."

"I look forward to getting to know them. Valerie, I know you've been a wonderful mother. I appreciate everything Joseph has done for you and them. I honestly wondered if the two of you married and had your own children."

"No, Ender. That wasn't an option. I knew once I was in love with you, there would never be another man for me. I have to tell you something, though." Valerie stops in the middle of the hallway and looks down at the floor. "I can't have any more children." Her voice breaks on the word children.

Ender wraps his arms around her and pulls her close. "I think two is enough for us, don't you?" Valerie cries silently as Ender holds her and guides her back to her room. Back in the room, Valerie clings to Ender as he lets her cry. It feels wonderful to be in his arms once again.

When her sobs subside, Ender releases her and takes a small step backward so he can look at her. He takes one of her hands and places it on his heart. The other hand lifts her chin to look at him.

"I'm all yours, baby. I will live with whatever decision you make about us as long as I can be in our children's lives." Valerie nods. Then Ender says the words he said years ago. "I'm bored waiting for you to ask me." He leans down and gently kisses Valerie's beautiful cupid bow lips. Valerie responds immediately by kissing him back with the love she had hidden away for so long.

The nurse interrupts the tender moment by coming into the room to tell Valerie she needs to return to bed. That night, Ender stays beside Valerie's bed so Joseph and Andrew can have time alone.

Early the following day, Joseph and Andrew arrive at the hospital. They have packed the vehicles for the trip back to Marfa. Ender kisses Valerie's cheek goodbye as the doctor gives her a sedative to make her sleep on the drive home. Ender and Andrew leave as soon as Valerie falls asleep.

Andrew drives while Ender sleeps. He wakes Ender when they reach at the house. Joseph texts Ender that he and Valerie are an hour away. The nanny is at the home with the twins when Ender and Andrew pull into the driveway.

"Papa! Papa!" the twins yell when they see Ender, and they run to him. Ender kneels and wraps them in his arms as tears fall from his eyes. After a few seconds, they force him to let them go as they wiggle their way out of his arms. Each twin takes one of Ender's hands, leading him to the backyard and their wooden blocks. The three of them are still working hard at building a castle when Joseph pulls up with Valerie.

"Mama! Mama!" the boy and girl scream as they run to the car. Ender follows and watches as Valerie opens the door and hugs them tightly.

"Okay, Sean and Sophie, papa needs to carry mama inside and put her to bed," Ender says with a huge grin. The twins turn and run into the house. Ender gently ifts Valerie out of the car and carries her to her bedroom. "That sounded pretty good to me," Ender murmurs in Valerie's ear.

"Ender, I'm supposed to walk," Valerie laughs.

"I know, but it has been so long since I carried you in my arms, I couldn't resist," he replies again, whispering in her ear as he nibbles her earlobe.

When Ender and Valerie reach the bedroom, he lies her on the bed. "Mama, papa has been building a castle with us in the backyard," the boy Sean says excitedly. Ender beams with pride.

"Well, I'll come out and see it in a few minutes. Sophie, did you work on the castle, too?" Sophie nods and reaches for Ender's hand. "Sean, would you get mama a glass of water? Sophie, go help your brother." Both children run out of the room.

"So far, so good," Ender says, sitting on the side of the bed. "Now, if only their mother were as easy to satisfy." Valerie places her head on the back of his neck and pulls him to her.

"Well, you could start with one of those delicious kisses, and I'm asking," she whispers.

The following two months fly by. Valerie graduates from cardiac rehab after one month and receives a clean bill of health from her doctor. Ender and Andrew work from their hotel rooms during the day. Ender spends evenings with Valerie and the twins, while Andrew and Joseph spend time together.

"Valerie, the grand opening of the hotel is Friday. Would you like to come with me?"

"No, Ender. This is a monumental accomplishment for you, and I don't want to distract you. So you and Andrew go and have a good time."

"Okay. I'll be back late on Sunday night. I'll miss you while I'm gone."

Chapter 55

Ender

Ender sent Andrew back to Marfa early Saturday morning, which surprised everyone, especially Andrew. So when Ender arrived at the hotel late Sunday night, he was alone and exhausted. He didn't even bother to turn the lights on in the room. Instead, Ender just stripped off his clothes and climbed into bed.

"I've been waiting for you," a sultry voice whispers.

"Baby, what a wonderful surprise," Ender says, taking Valerie into his arms and kissing her. The kissing becomes very hot and passionate. Then, suddenly, Ender pulls back. "Who's with the kids?"

"Joseph and Andrew are there," Valerie answers.

"Baby, are you well enough?"

"I wouldn't be here if I wasn't. Now, will you talk all night or make me yours again?"

Ender lies on his side, facing Valerie long after the sun has risen. He watches her sleep, knowing the night of lovemaking wore her out. Ender brushes the hair from her face and smiles. Then he carefully gets out of bed, walks to his messenger bag, and removes a small velvet box. He gets back into bed and hides the box under his pillow. Ender knows he's taking an enormous risk but believes it is time.

Valerie opens her eyes and smiles at Ender several minutes later. "Hi, beautiful," Ender says, kissing softly on the tip of her nose. "How did you sleep?"

"I slept like I was where I was meant to be. With you in your arms," Valerie answers, stretching.

Ender watches as the sheet pulls away from her body as she stretches. When he sees the scar from the C-section, he leans over and tenderly kisses the scar from one end to the other. Then he leans on one elbow and looks at Valerie.

"You went through a lot giving birth to our babies. I'm sorry I wasn't there for you." He reaches under the pillow and pulls out the box. Ender watches Valerie watching him. He opens the box. "Valerie, I want to share everything with you for the rest of our lives if you will have me. I love you beyond words. Will you marry me?"

"Yes! Yes! Yes!" Valerie shouts at the top of her lungs. Ender slips the ring on her finger and pulls her into his arms.

"How long can Andrew and Joseph stay with the twins?" he asks breathlessly.

"Until I get home whenever that is. Who cares?" Valerie whispers.

Chapter 56

Valerie

I do not know what's happening with anyone; lately, Valerie thinks. Ender's gone more than before and fired Andrew. Andrew and Joseph got married at the courthouse and then left for two weeks, telling no one where they were going. I think Ender knows where they went, but he won't talk about it. So now, Ender wants to have a family meeting tonight when he gets back.

At least while Ender was gone, Valerie could go to the courthouse and have the twins' birth certificates changed to the last name of Dogan and Ender listed as their father. Valerie also got the twins' passports, hoping to take them to Istanbul one day.

Finally, Ender pulls up in the driveway and walks into the house. "Family meeting in the living room," he yells. Valerie gathers the twins and heads to the room. "Where's the rest of the family?" Ender asks. He stomps out of the house. Minutes later, he, Andrew, and Joseph appear. Ender has an angry look on his face and points for Andrew and Joseph to sit down. "From now on, when I say we're going to have a family meeting, I intend for all of you to attend because you are all my family." He then grins, insisting everyone stand for a group hug.

"Now, the real reason for the meeting. Valerie is well enough to travel now. She and I haven't talked about this, so I'm sure this will shock her." Ender looks at Valerie with a sheepish look on his face. "I want to take Valerie and the twins home. By home, I mean to Istanbul."

The announcement catches Valerie off guard momentarily. "Ender, I think that's a wonderful idea. There's nothing to keep us in the US but your business. You've proven that you can run it from wherever you are. I want Sean and Sophie to grow up knowing your native language and culture."

"I'm happy you feel that way, Valerie. Now, what are your thoughts, Andrew and Joseph?"

"Well, Andrew and I have been talking," Joseph begins. "There's really nothing here for us either, so we went to Istanbul looking for houses in your neighborhood."

"Why do I get the feeling I'm the last to know about this?" Valerie asks.

"I want to go to Itthanbel," Sean says, causing everyone to laugh.

"What about you, Sophie? Do you want to go to Istanbul?" Ender asks.

"Do they have baby dolls?" Sophie asks.

"Of course they do, sweetheart," Ender answers, kneeling in front of her. "If they don't have the ones you want, mama and I will get them for you."

Sophie throws her arms around Ender. "Okay, papa. Let's go."

Ender picks her up and walks to the center of the room. He reaches into his pocket and pulls out a set of keys. "Joseph and Andrew, I understand you found a house about one-half mile from ours and fell in love with it." Both men nod. Ender tosses the keys at them. "Here's your wedding gift from Valerie and me."

"Really?" Andrew asks. Ender nods while Valerie cries.

"Now, the question is, how soon can we get there? Any suggestions, family?"

"Andrew and I can leave within two weeks," Joseph says. "I have someone that wants to buy everything and start his own business."

"I just have to pack out clothes," Valerie says. "We can leave anytime you want, Ender."

"Fine," Ender says with a massive grin. "Valerie and I will leave at the end of the week. I'll send the jet back to pick you up whenever the two of you are ready." He looks at Andrew and Joseph, who nod enthusiastically.

Chapter 57

Ender

Three months later, Ender, Valerie, and the twins have settled into life at home in Istanbul. Ender hired a tutor to teach the kids and Valerie the Turkish language and brush himself up. In addition, Ender makes two trips to Miami during the three months and goes into his Istanbul office once a week.

Andrew and Joseph have settled into their new home and have been looking into adoption. However, since Turkey does not recognize same-sex marriages, they have run into problems. Refusing to give up, Andrew and Joseph searched for a set of twins the same age as Sean and Sophie and found a set. They have been fostering the kids for one month and have fallen in love with them.

One Saturday morning, Ender and Valerie wake up wrapped in each other's arms. "Good morning, baby," Ender says. "Do you have plans for the day?" Valerie shakes her head, wiggles her eyebrows, and snuggles against him.

Two hours later, the couple climbs out of bed and showers together. As they walk into the bedroom, Ender announces, "today, we are doing something totally different. Trust me on this."

"Okay, Ender, I'll do whatever you want."

"Good girl," he says, nuzzling her neck. "Close your eyes tightly." Valerie does while Ender walks into his closet and retrieves a necktie. He ties it around Valerie's eyes. Next, Ender goes into her closet and gets underwear, a dress, and sandals. He dresses her carefully and tenderly.

Valerie giggles when he puts her underwear on. "It's different putting it on instead of taking it off, isn't it, Ender?"

"I didn't realize there was so much work involved," he replies, tickling her. "Now, I'm going to sit you down on the bed while I dress." When he's finished, Ender grabs his phone and sends a quick text message receiving a thumbs-up emoji in response.

"Time to stand up, baby," Ender tells Valerie as he takes her hands and pulls her to her feet. Then he bends and picks her up. He carries her into the garden and looks around to ensure everything is ready. Finally, Ender sets Valerie down and removes the necktie with her facing the inside of the house.

Valerie gasps in surprise when she sees their reflections in the glass. She and Ender are dressed in white. Ender slowly turns her around. The garden is in full bloom and beautiful. A white carpet leads the way to an arch covered in jasmine. Under the arch stands a government official in his uniform. To the official's left stands Joseph, Sean, and the male twin Joseph and Andrew are fostering. To the right stands Andrew, Sophie, and the female twin the men are fostering. Everyone is standing there dressed in white.

"Baby, I believe you agreed to marry me," Ender whispers in Valerie's ear.

"I did," she replies.

"Shall we?" Ender asks, offering her his arm.

Together, they walk down the carpet to the arch. The ceremony is brief, and the official announces the groom can now kiss his bride.

"Not yet," Ender says. "I believe it is customary for the groom to give his bride a wedding gift." He looks down at his beautiful wife. "My gift to you is that I have sold everything except the house and cars. I'm all yours today and always."

"I have a gift for you, but it's in my purse," Valerie says, looking around. Andrew touches her arm and hands her an envelope. Valerie opens the envelope and hands the papers to Ender. "Here are Sean and Sophie's birth certificates naming you as their father and officially giving them your last name." Valerie wipes the tears from Ender's face as all four kids begin jumping and yelling, "kiss, kiss, kiss"!

Ender holds up his hand. "I have one more thing." The government official hands Ender two envelopes. "Andrew and Joseph, with laws being the way they are, I couldn't make things perfect, but here are your adoption papers for the twins. Joseph, you adopted the boy, and Andrew, you adopted the girl." He hands each one their envelopes.

"Now my family is complete, and I can kiss my wife," Ender says, pulling Valerie to him.

Gaylene Nunn is a widowed 60+ year old woman who spent her career in banking, financial services, municipal government, and most recently as CFO for a upper level regional university that she helped create. She retired in 2017 with the title of Vice President Emeritus. Gaylene is a Texas native who enjoys reading, writing, traveling, and spending time with her dog, Sam, and cat, Emily.

Gaylene Nunn

Before Your Loved Ones Goes—Planning for Your Reality

Forty Years Too Late

Reclaimed Assurance

Deserie LaCrosse & Gaylene Nunn

An Eternity of Love

Damaged by Love